Claudia and the Recipe for Danger

**Other books by
Ann M. Martin**

Rachel Parker, Kindergarten Show-off

Eleven Kids, One Summer

Ma and Pa Dracula

Yours Turly, Shirley

Ten Kids, No Pets

Slam Book

Just a Summer Romance

Missing Since Monday

With You and Without You

Me and Katie (the Pest)

Stage Fright

Inside Out

Bummer Summer

BABY-SITTERS LITTLE SISTER series
THE BABY-SITTERS CLUB mysteries
THE BABY-SITTERS CLUB series

THE BABY-SITTERS CLUB

Claudia and the Recipe for Danger

Ann M. Martin

AN
APPLE
PAPERBACK

SCHOLASTIC INC.
New York Toronto London Auckland Sydney

Cover art by Hodges Soileau

No part of this publication may be reproduced in whole or in part, or stored in a retrieval system, or transmitted in any form or by any means, electronic, mechanical, photocopying, recording, or otherwise, without written permission of the publisher. For information regarding permission, write to Scholastic Inc., 555 Broadway, New York, NY 10012.

ISBN 0-590-48310-2

12 11 10 9 8 7 6 5 4 3 2 1   5 6 7 8 9/9 0/0

Printed in the U.S.A.   40

First Scholastic printing, August 1995

The author gratefully acknowledges
Ellen Miles
for her help in
preparing this manuscript.

Famous for your French bread?
Adored for your apple pie?
Chased after for your cheesecake?

———————— **Enter the** ————————

MRS. GOODE'S COOKWARE BATTLE OF THE BAKERS

and be rewarded for your excellent baking skills!

Two age groups (9–15 years and 16– adult) will compete in a four-day contest, to be held over two weekends. First Prize winners in each group will receive

———— $1,000.00 ————

And both First Prize recipes wil be printed in the new
MRS. GOODE'S COOKWARE COOKBOOK.

Contestants may enter as either individuals or teams. Team size is limited to three people. The first three days of the contest will be considered preliminary rounds. At the end of three days, our distinguished judges will choose the finalists, who will compete on the fourth day. Contestants may use the same recipe each day or use different recipes for each round. Time limit for each round: three hours. Recipes will be judged on appearance as well as taste.

The Battle of the Bakers will be held in the gymnasium of Stoneybrook High School. Mrs. Goode's cookware will be available and *must* be used. Free day care will be provided for children of contestants.

Enter now!
Space is limited to ten slots for each contest!

CHAPTER 1

"Crayon, book, bird, candy — mmm, candy!" said Jamie, fingering each piece as he named it and then pretending to take a bite out of the tiny silver Hershey's Kiss that dangles from my bracelet. It's a charm bracelet, just like the ones most people wear on their wrists. I like to be a little different, so I wear mine on my ankle.

At the moment, that ankle was dangling over a foot of cool water. I was sitting on the ground, leaning back on my elbows, with both feet hanging over the edge of Jamie Newton's Lion King wading pool.

No, Jamie isn't my boyfriend. (I actually don't have a boyfriend at the moment. Know any cool, single guys?) He's cute, but he's way, way too young for me. Jamie's only four years old. That wading pool, while it looks the size of a puddle to me, must seem like a full-size Olympic pool to him. He was splashing

1

happily in it, stopping every few seconds to hitch up his red-and-blue-striped bathing suit, which threatened to fall down around his ankles every time he moved.

I was baby-sitting for Jamie while his mom took his baby sister Lucy to the pediatrician. He'd been in the pool ever since she left, and I was glad to hang out and watch him, even though it meant being splashed every few minutes. Those sprays of water felt great, because it was *hot* outside. That's right, *hot*. Not just warm. Not just hot. *HOT!* It was midsummer, and it was the kind of day when you work up a sweat just sitting still. So I felt happy to be hanging out under the big maple tree in the Newtons' frontyard, with my feet over the pool and a white baseball cap pulled down low over my eyes.

I guess it's about time for me to tell you who I am. My name is Claudia Kishi, I'm thirteen years old, and my charm bracelet is my life. No, seriously. I've chosen the charms carefully to represent different parts of my personality. You can learn a lot about me by studying each charm in turn.

For example, the little crayon symbolizes my love for art of all kinds. I love creating art, looking at it, learning about it, and even just thinking about it. Art is a major part of my life.

The bird that Jamie was looking at is a silver crane, which represents my Japanese heritage. In Japan, the crane is a symbol of peace. I'm Japanese-American: both of my parents are, too. You'd know it if you looked at me, since I have dark, almond-shaped eyes and long, straight, shiny black hair. I look almost exactly like my grandmother Mimi did when she was my age. She came to this country from Japan when she was thirty-two years old. Mimi lived with my family until she died not long ago, and I was very close to her. Looking at the little crane on my charm bracelet always reminds me of her, and makes me feel proud of my ancestry.

The Hershey's Kiss stands for my devotion to junk food. But that devotion is by no means limited to chocolate. No, I make it a point to eat a balanced junk-food diet, choosing each day from the four official junk-food groups: candy, chips, cookies, and soda. My parents don't approve (they believe in those other, totally boring food groups: dairy, meat, grains, and vegetables), so I keep my addiction a secret.

The book charm reveals another of my secrets: I adore Nancy Drew mysteries. My parents would prefer that I read the literary equivalent of the four food groups, so the Nancy Drews are currently hidden in my sock drawer along with the Snickers bars and Fritos. I'm pretty good about not reading them when I should be doing other things, such as homework.

I go to Stoneybrook Middle School — when school's in session, that is. School is my favorite thing in the whole world. Not! Truthfully, school is something I could probably live without pretty easily, except for the fact that I'd miss my friends. Well, I'd miss art class, too, I guess. But, that day by Jamie's pool, even though I was starting to feel the tiniest bit bored with the long, hot days of summer, I definitely wasn't eager for school to start again.

My older sister Janine, on the other hand, is one of those kids who can't get enough school. She's a junior in high school, but she also takes college classes. (She's a genius, so she can handle it.) I've actually seen her act all mopey on the last day of school, because she hates to "bid the academic year farewell," as she once put it. Not that summer makes much of a difference in her routine. To Janine, free time is just time to fill up with classes and seminars and reading and studying. Her boyfriend Jerry practically has to beg her to take time off for picnics and hikes.

My parents, naturally, are very proud of Janine. But you know what? Even though they have to nag me about doing my homework on time, they're proud of me, too. They're supportive, they're enthusiastic about my art, and they're impressed by the fact that I've been earning all my own spending money for a long time now.

I do that by baby-sitting, which is one of my other loves. (Maybe I should buy a little baby rattle or something to add to my charm bracelet.) I belong to a club — well, really, it's more like a business — called the Baby-sitters Club, or BSC. All of us in the club love kids and love taking care of them, which is why our club has been so successful.

"Look, Claudee!"

I had been lost in my thoughts, but Jamie's cry made me jump to my feet just in time to avoid being completely soaked by a miniature tidal wave he had stirred up. "Yow!" I yelled, as the water sloshed over the sides of the pool.

Jamie giggled and hitched up his suit. Then, suddenly, he frowned. "I'm tired of swimming," he announced.

Kids' moods change so suddenly sometimes.

"Okay," I said agreeably. "Why don't you hop out so I can dry you off? Then we'll think of something else to do."

Jamie climbed out of the pool and let me wrap him up in a soft, fresh-smelling blue towel. He squirmed like a puppy while I dried his hair, and I couldn't resist giving him a little squeeze.

Once Jamie was dry, I emptied out the pool and left it upside-down, which was what Mrs. Newton had asked me to do. I would have done it anyway, since I know that even a shallow pool full of water can be dangerous for young kids. Then we headed inside to find dry clothes (for Jamie) and a drink of water (for me).

Jamie dresses slowly. He's at that stage when he wants to do everything himself, even though he's not great yet at things such as buckles and buttons and shoelaces. Still, he managed to put everything on right-side out and front-side forward, while I sat on his bed, watching and thinking about what we could do next.

I toyed with my ankle bracelet while I waited, and felt one more charm I'd almost forgotten about. It was a tiny silver rectangle, a miniature replica of a credit card. My friend and fellow BSC member Stacey McGill gave it to me, and it symbolizes my love for shopping. Stacey just happens to be my number-one shopping partner. She grew up in New York City and has an incredible sense of style. We have different tastes. She's mondo sophisticated, while I'm more into funky outfits and creative accessorizing. But when I'm ready to cruise the aisles hunting for bargains, there's nobody I'd rather have along than Stacey.

"Stacey!" I said out loud. "That's it."

"What?" asked Jamie, who was trying to straighten out the pockets on his shorts.

"Stacey is sitting for Charlotte today," I said. "Remember Stacey?"

Jamie nodded. He hadn't seen Stacey for a while, because she hadn't been sitting much. She was kicked out of the BSC temporarily, which is a long story, but now she's a member again and she's starting to take on sitting jobs once more. Actually, she never did stop sitting for Charlotte Johanssen, mainly because Charlotte and Stacey, who are both only children, are so close that they think of themselves as "almost sisters."

Jamie was waiting for me to explain why I'd mentioned Stacey.

"How about if we go over to Charlotte's and see if she and Stacey would like to take a walk downtown with us?" I asked him.

"Yea!" said Jamie. "Can we have an ice cream?"

"Ice cream!" I said, grinning. "Yuck! How about liver, instead?"

Jamie shrieked with laughter. "No! Ice

cream," he said, jumping up and down.

"Oh, all right," I said. "I just thought you'd rather have liver."

Jamie laughed some more. Kids love wacky things like that. And I love to say them. Sometimes I think my sense of humor never developed much past the four-year-old stage.

Soon Jamie was all set, and after leaving a note for Mrs. Newton, we headed over to the Johannsens' to pick up Charlotte and Stacey. (I'd called ahead to see if they were interested in coming with us, and they were.) Then the four of us started out for downtown, with Charlotte and Jamie leading the way and Stacey and I following behind.

"Charlotte adores Jamie," Stacey said.

The two of them were walking hand in hand, and Charlotte was looking after Jamie as if *she* were his baby-sitter.

"He loves her, too," I said, smiling at Stacey. It sure felt good to be hanging out with her again. Things had really cooled off between us while she was out of the BSC, but they were starting to return to normal now, and I was glad.

We chatted all the way downtown. And it seemed like old times when we went into Merry-Go-Round together, trailing after Jamie and Charlotte, who were curious about a display of teddy-bear jewelry. Merry-Go-Round is one of my favorite stores: it's crammed with fun, inexpensive accessories and jewelry. Stacey's always loved it, too. We browsed for fifteen minutes or so, until the kids were ready to leave. Then we strolled down the sidewalk, window-shopping, talking, and giggling. We walked past Bellair's department store, where Stacey's mom works, and Stacey told me about a new brand of jeans they'd be carrying soon.

Then we stopped to read the bulletin board at Pizza Express. That's where I first learned about the Battle of the Bakers. Stacey spotted the sign, and pointed it out to me. "That looks like fun," she said.

I looked at the sign. "Mrs. Goode's Cookware sponsors the Battle of the Bakers," I read out loud. "Two age groups — nine to fifteen and sixteen and over — will compete as individuals or in teams over two weekends for prizes of up to one thousand dollars!"

"Wow!" said Charlotte. "That's a lot of money."

"Plus, the winners are going to be in the new Mrs. Goode's cookbook," Stacey added, pointing to the sign.

"Cupcakes!" said Jamie. "That's what *my* mommy bakes." He rubbed his stomach and looked wistful.

That reminded me that we had promised the kids ice cream, so after I took one more

CHAPTER 2

"Ta-daaaa!" I cried. I held up two plates, each piled high with goodies.

My friends applauded.

"Mmm, those look good," said Mallory, licking her lips. "Brownies?"

"Nope," I said. "No more brownies out of a box for me. I'm practicing for the Battle of the Bakers. These are something special." I held out the plate in my right hand to Kristy, who was leaning back in the director's chair by my desk. "Madame President?" I said, bowing. She helped herself.

Then I went around the room, offering the plate in my right hand to Mal, Mary Anne, and Jessi. When I came to Stacey and Dawn, I offered them the plate in my left hand. "Just for you," I said, winking at them.

The room was quiet for a second while everyone savored their first bites. Then Kristy gave a little cough. "Very good, Claud," she said. I didn't see her taking another bite, though. "And they're so beautiful," added Mary Anne. "Just look at the way this icing is dribbled. It looks like marble."

I beamed. That was just the effect I'd been trying for. "They're mocha-walnut fudge dream bars," I said. "My own recipe." I paused. "Oh — and the ones I gave you guys," I added, turning to Dawn and Stacey, who were looking a little shocked, "were carrot walnut dream bars. Sweetened with fruit juice." Stacey looked relieved, and so did Dawn. Neither of them eats junk food, which is why I'd made a special batch of treats just for them.

I'd rushed into the kitchen as soon as I'd arrived home from sitting for Jamie the day before. I couldn't wait to try out some ideas I had been thinking about ever since I had seen the sign for the baking contest. I planned on having a taste test when everyone came to my house for our Wednesday BSC meeting.

But something was wrong. Nobody was scarfing down their treats. I grabbed one and sat down on the bed to eat it. As soon as I took one bite, I knew what the problem was. It tasted like salted cardboard.

The dream bars were a nightmare.

"Yuck!" I said, putting it down. "Oh, well," I added, shrugging. "They *looked* great." To me, looks mean a lot. I'd just have to work on the recipe a little, maybe pay a bit more attention to measurements and things.

"Luckily, I have back-up snacks," I said, pulling some strawberry fruit leather out from under the bed and tossing it to Kristy. Next I poked under my pillow and found a package of Twizzlers, which I handed down to Mal. Finally, I dug around in my night table drawer until I found a bag of Smartfood I'd been saving. I passed it over to Dawn and Stacey, who were sitting next to me on the bed.

"Just in time," said Kristy, glancing at my clock, which had just clicked over to five-thirty. "I sheerfy fall viz phweeting phoo morger," she added.

"What?" I asked. We all started laughing.

Kristy chewed and swallowed. "Sorry," she said. "What I meant was, I hereby call this meeting to order."

Kristy — that's Kristy Thomas — is president of the BSC, as you might have guessed by now. That's because it was her idea to start with. Kristy is a real idea person, and she's great at putting her ideas into action. The BSC is one of her simplest and best ideas. Here's how it works: the club meets in my room three times a week, Mondays, Wednesdays, and Fridays, from five-thirty until six. I have my own phone line (that's how I became vice-president!), and parents can call my number during those times to set up sitting jobs. Since there are seven of us, plus two associate members, someone is always available. At first we advertised, with classified ads and fliers, but now we hardly ever have to. Satisfied clients are our best advertising, as Kristy often says.

If I had a charm bracelet with charms that symbolized each of my friends in the BSC, the Kristy charm would have to be a baseball. That charm would represent Kristy's love of sports, and also her energy and enthusiasm for organizing things. Besides running the BSC, she's also founder and manager of Kristy's Krushers, a softball team for little kids.

Kristy is on the short side, with brown hair and brown eyes. She doesn't care much about fashion. Her idea of a terrific accessory is her baseball cap with the picture of a collie on it. But here's what Kristy does care about: people. Especially kids. Kristy comes from a big, close-knit family. She has two older brothers, Charlie and Sam; a younger brother, David Michael; a stepbrother named Andrew, and a stepsister named Karen (both younger), who live with Kristy's family every other month; and an adopted baby sister named Emily Michelle. There are also some pets: a puppy named Shannon, a cat named Boo-Boo, a couple of goldfish and, during the months when

Karen and Andrew are around, a rat and a hermit crab. When the whole family (including Nannie, Kristy's grandmother) is together in Watson Brewer's mansion (Watson is Kristy's stepfather, and he's a millionaire), you can hardly hear yourself think!

Somehow, though, Kristy still manages to. Think, that is. Since she started the BSC, she's come up with plenty of ideas that help make it the best club — and the best baby-sitting business — ever. For instance, Kid-Kits, which are portable boxes full of toys (mostly hand-me-downs, but kids love them), stickers, and art supplies. My Kid-Kit has saved my life on more than one rainy-day sitting job. Kristy also invented the club notebook, in which we each write up every job we go on. This helps us stay on top of what's going on with our regular clients, and I think the parents appreciate that kind of special attention. Writing in the notebook is not my favorite activity — it's a little too much like homework — but I still have to admit it's a good idea.

Another patented Kristy invention is the club record book, in which we keep information (from addresses to allergies) on all of our clients. In it, we also keep track of our schedules, so we know who's available for what job. Mary Anne Spier, the BSC secretary, is in charge of the record book. Mary Anne is one of my oldest friends, but she's Kristy's best friend, even though they're not much alike. Kristy is level-headed and can be a little bossy, and Mary Anne is emotional and very shy. (The two of them do *look* a little bit alike. Mary Anne is short, with brown hair and brown eyes just like Kristy's. But Mary Anne is more interested in fashion, plus she has a cool haircut.) Mary Anne's charm on my BSC bracelet would have to be a kitten, which would symbolize her soft heart and sweet nature, and also her beloved pet Tigger.

Since her mom died when Mary Anne was just a baby, Mr. Spier brought Mary Anne up by himself. For years he was majorly strict, but he's eased up lately, partly because he's learned that Mary Anne is a responsible, mature person, and partly (we all think) because he married again not long ago. He married Sharon Schafer, his high school sweetheart, who had moved to California after graduation, and gotten married to someone else. She came back to Stoneybrook when she divorced her husband and, as Mary Anne puts it, the old flame was rekindled.

Mary Anne had a hand in reigniting that fire. It just so happened that Sharon Schafer brought two kids with her from California, Dawn and her younger brother Jeff. Dawn and Mary Anne became immediate best friends, discovered that their parents used to date, fixed them up again, and ended up as stepsisters (to make a long story short). Dawn is a BSC member, too, naturally. She's the alternate officer, which means she can fill in for any other officer who can't make it to a meeting. For example, she filled in for Stacey when Stacey was out of the club.

Dawn is cool. She has long, long pale blonde hair, eyes so blue they look like swimming pools, a clear, clear complexion that must be due partly to her extremely healthy eating habits (tofu and veggies — ugh!), and an attitude that's totally laid back. To me, Dawn will always look as if she belongs on a beach. Her charm on my bracelet? No question. A pair of sunglasses.

Dawn has learned to love Stoneybrook, but her brother Jeff never did adjust to life on the East Coast. He ended up going back to California to live with his dad. And not long ago, Dawn realized she missed them both so much that she needed to go out there for an extended visit. She's back with us now, but I can tell she's already homesick again for California and the people she loves out there. Plus, she just had some pretty bad news about the mother of her best friend in California, and I know it's hard for Dawn to feel so far away.

When I think of split-up lives, I also think

of Stacey. Her parents are divorced, and her dad lives in Manhattan, where Stacey grew up. (Her charm would definitely be a miniature Empire State Building.) She visits him as often as possible (always managing to slip into Bloomingdale's or have her long blonde hair permed while she's in the city), but I know she misses having her family together.

Stacey's life is also split up because she's pulled in different directions by us, her friends in the BSC, and by her boyfriend Robert Brewster. Remember when I mentioned that she had been temporarily kicked out of the club? Well, that was because she became overly involved with Robert and his friends and she blew off her BSC friends — and responsibilities. We know she's crazy about Robert, but if she wants to be a part of this club she needs to put in time with us, too.

Things can't be easy for Stacey, but I think she's beginning to learn how to balance the parts of her life. Stacey's already mastered one tricky balancing act, and I really admire her for it. She's a diabetic, which means that her body can't manage sugar properly. She has to take extra good care of herself — give herself insulin injections every day and also watch what she eats. (That's why I made her those fruit-juice-sweetened carrot bars.)

Stacey is treasurer of the BSC and, math

whiz that she is, she does a great job of it. She keeps track of every dollar we earn, and also collects dues every Monday, which go toward things such as my phone bill and Kristy's transportation costs (which is a fancy way of saying that we buy gas for her brother Charlie, who drives her to meetings).

I know Stacey's happy to be back in the BSC, but she's a little nervous about it, too. She's on probation, and I think everyone, especially Kristy, is watching her closely to make sure she "behaves."

Okay. Everybody I've told you about so far is thirteen and in the eighth grade. But two members of the BSC are eleven and in the sixth grade. They are Jessi Ramsey and Mallory Pike, and they happen to be best friends. They're junior officers, which means they can't baby-sit at night unless it's for their own siblings.

Jessi's charm on the BSC bracelet would be a toe shoe. She's an amazing ballet dancer, and I bet she'll be internationally famous when she's older. Jessi has other interests beside dancing, though; like Mal, she loves horses and loves to read. (Naturally, she and Mal like horse stories best.) And she loves her family: her parents, her aunt Cecelia, her little sister Becca, and her baby brother Squirt. (His real name is John Philip Ramsey, Jr., but I have a feeling he'll be Squirt when he's ninety!) The Ramseys are African-American, and they didn't receive the greatest reception when they moved to Stoneybrook not long ago. But now they're as much a part of the community as anyone else.

Mal's family is a community all by itself! She has seven younger brothers and sisters, which is one reason she's a great baby-sitter. She's looked after Adam, Jordan, Byron (they're triplets), Vanessa, Nicky, Margo, and Claire for as long as she can remember. Mal's charm on the BSC bracelet? Let's see. How about a pencil, to represent her future career as a writer and illustrator of children's books? I can't wait to see her picture on a book jacket. Mal's going to be a knockout one day when she grows into her looks. For now, she hates her reddish-brown hair, braces, and glasses with a passion.

Remember those two associate members I mentioned? They help out when we're way busy, and their names are Logan Bruno and Shannon Kilbourne. Logan is Mary Anne's steady boyfriend and he's a great guy. I think a soccer ball would make a good charm for Logan, since he's great at sports. And Shannon is a smart, friendly girl from Kristy's neighborhood. (She gave the Thomases their puppy, and they named it after her.)

I was busy trying to think of a charm for Shannon (maybe those sad-and-happy masks, to symbolize her being in the drama club?) when I heard the phone ring. I grabbed it. "Hello, Baby-sitters Club," I said. I listened while the caller explained what he wanted, told him I'd call him back, and turned to my friends. I had exciting news.

"That was somebody from the Mrs. Goode's baking contest," I said. "His name's Marty Nisson, and check this out! He wants to know if we could run an on-site day-care center to take care of contestants' kids during the days of the contest. The contest is going to be held in the high school gym, and we'd be in the faculty lounge. He says we were 'highly recommended'!"

"Of course!" said Kristy.

"Let's do it!" said Mal and Jessi.

"Sounds like fun," said Stacey. "I know Mr. Johanssen wants to enter, and I'm sure he'd appreciate having a place for Charlotte to stay in."

"Same with Mrs. Newton," I said. "She told me she's planning to enter."

Mary Anne checked the record book. "I think we could handle it," she said. "Even though I want to be *in* the contest, and so does Claudia."

Our meeting was almost over, so I called

Marty Nisson back and told him we'd be glad to handle the day care for the contest. By then it was six, so Kristy declared the meeting adjourned, but nobody seemed ready to leave the room. Mary Anne and I pored over the flier I had brought home, checking out all the rules and regulations for the Battle of the Bakers, while Kristy, Stacey, Mal, Jessi, and Dawn started talking excitedly about the day-care center. August was shaping up to be an interesting month.

CHAPTER 3

I threw down one *Chocolate Lover's* magazine, picked up another, and started to flip through it. "Hey, check this out," I said, taking a closer look at a full-page color picture of one of the most beautiful cakes I'd ever seen. It was covered in white chocolate icing and trimmed with cascades of flowers in all shades of purple and pink, with this lacy golden stuff on top. I read the caption and discovered that the golden stuff was spun sugar. "What a gorgeous cake," I said, sighing. "No way the judges could ignore something like *that*."

It was Thursday, over a week after the BSC meeting at which we'd first discussed the Battle of the Bakers. The contest was to start on Saturday, so there wasn't too much time left for deciding on a recipe.

Mary Anne put down the Fannie Farmer cookbook she was leafing through and looked over my shoulder. "It's pretty, Claud," she

23

said, "but don't you think it looks a little hard to make?" She pointed to the caption below a picture, on the opposite page, of a tall, skinny man in a tall, puffy white hat. " 'Master Chef Pierre Fontainbleu, creator of this recipe, reveals every secret in his ten-day process,' " she read.

"Ten days!" said Shea Rodowsky, who had been sitting quietly at my desk, looking through a stack of *Gourmet* magazines. "No way. We don't even have ten *hours*. We have to come up with a recipe we can make in one morning."

"Shea's right," Mary Anne said. "Let's keep looking. I'm sure we can figure out something that will be quick and delicious." She glanced at me. "And beautiful," she added quickly.

I sighed. I knew Mary Anne and Shea were right, but somehow it was hard for me to give up my dream of baking some outrageously gorgeous creation, one that would knock the judges' eyes out. After all, I'm an artist, not a chef.

Mary Anne patted my hand. "Come on, Claud," she said. "We're a team, remember? We can do it if we all work together."

I smiled at her. "You're right, Mary Anne. Soon we'll be splitting up that prize money. We are a team!"

We had turned into a team only recently,

24

so I was just becoming used to the idea. But I knew it was a good one. We'd have a much better chance if we worked together. I knew I was lucky to have Mary Anne, who does happen to know her way around a kitchen, and Shea, who's great with figures and measurements, on my team.

Mary Anne and I had agreed to be a team after Wednesday's BSC meeting, when we realized that we didn't want to compete against each other. The rule of the baking contest said that teams could consist of no more than three members each, but at that point we thought the two of us could manage just fine.

On Thursday, Logan decided to enter. He's a good cook, and he can be very competitive, so a cooking contest sounded great to him. He promised his little sister Kerry that she could be on his team, too, and he tried to talk Mary Anne into joining them, but she didn't want to abandon me. (She doesn't mind competing against Logan — in fact, they were recently on opposing teams for this zoo project we worked on for school.)

Then, on Friday, it turned out that Austin Bentley, who goes to SMS with us, was looking for a team to join. He ended up on Logan's team. Later, when Mrs. Rodowsky, one of our regular clients, announced she would enter the contest, her nine-year-old son Shea decided *he* wanted to be in it, too. She called the BSC on Monday to ask if we had a place for him.

I was happy to have Shea on my team, since he and I are old pals. Shea's dyslexic, and has trouble in school just like I do, except that he happens to have a natural talent for math. We've learned a lot from each other.

Mary Anne and I invited Shea to join our team, so the BSC teams were set with three members each.

I knew another team in the contest. Cokie Mason was on it, along with her friends Grace Blume and Mari Drabek. The three of them go to SMS, but they are not exactly friends of ours. Cokie is the worst. She gives me a pain. For some reason (jealousy, maybe?) she has always been out to ruin the BSC. She's constantly plotting and planning, hoping to trip us up whenever she can. (Not to mention that she once went so far as to try to steal Logan away from Mary Anne.)

Mary Anne and I ran into Cokie on Tuesday, when we were at the supermarket checking out prices on basic ingredients such as flour, sugar, baking powder, and baking chocolate. Cokie was fingering a package of butterscotch chips when she spotted us.

"Shopping for the contest?" she asked, with

26

that little Cokie sneer. "I don't know why you're bothering."

"We're bothering because we're going to win!" I said, narrowing my eyes at her. Mary Anne touched me on the shoulder, a signal to stay cool.

Cokie gave a snort. "Yeah, right," she said. "Like you have a chance. Listen, I'll give you a little tip right now. My team has a secret weapon, and nobody, I mean *nobody*, is going to beat us when it comes to impressing the judges." She folded her arms and gave us a smug look.

I started to say something, but Mary Anne grabbed me by the elbow and steered me away from Cokie. "Look, Claudia," she said. "What an excellent price on slivered almonds!"

When we were far enough away from Cokie, I hissed, "What do you think their secret weapon is?" I have to admit that I was dying of curiosity, even though I'd never let Cokie have the pleasure of knowing that.

"I doubt there is one," said Mary Anne. "She's just trying to psych us out."

Mary Anne was wrong. Cokie's team *did* have a secret weapon. But we didn't find out what it was until the next day, when my BSC friends and I went to the high school to meet with Marty Nisson and talk about the day-care center.

Marty turned out to be a college intern and a pretty nice guy. He was tall, with wavy black hair and wire-rimmed glasses — cute, but way too old for me and not really my type anyway. He seemed ultra-organized, and as he showed us the faculty lounge he explained what he would need from the BSC.

"The contest runs all day for both days over the next two weekends," he said. "We want to provide child care during both the adults' and kids' competitions. There'll be a lot more kids for you to watch in the morning, during the adult matches, but we think parents might want day care available in the afternoon, too, in case they need to go shopping for ingredients. Also, some of the out-of-towners may want to tour Stoneybrook. Anyway, we'll need sitters from eight to probably about five each day. It would be nice to have at least three or four of you here in the morning, though more would be fine, and maybe two of you in the afternoon. We'll pay you a flat fee for the four days, and you can split that however you want."

"Sounds fine," said Kristy.

Mary Anne was making notes in the record book, which she'd brought along.

"Also," added Marty, "I'll need one of you to help out as a Cake Cop during the afternoon competitions."

"Cake Cop?" I repeated, giggling. "What's that for, to give tickets to people who steal icing or something?"

Marty looked dead serious. "Nope," he said. "It's somebody who helps me make sure that no rules are broken, and that nobody tries to cheat. This contest is pretty important to some people, and we want to make sure it's run right. For example, if any adult was caught helping a younger baker, that baker or team would be disqualified."

"Oh," I said. I wasn't giggling anymore.

"I'd love to be a Cake Cop," Kristy said. "I can be available whenever you need me."

"Great," said Marty. "Now, how about if I show you the setup in the gym?" He led us down the hall.

I've been in the SHS gym before, but it had never looked like *this*. Ten gleaming white stove-and-counter combinations were set up in two rows of five each, with shoulder-high dividers between them. A judge's table had been set up under one of the basketball hoops. Marty was in the midst of explaining that extra sinks had been installed in the locker rooms when I spotted Grace Blume. She and some other people were wandering around the gym, scoping out the equipment.

"Grace," I said, catching up to her a few

minutes later as soon as we'd finished with Marty, "where's Cokie?"

"She's home," said Grace miserably. "With a terrible case of bronchitis. She's coughing all over the place, and her mom says she can't be in the contest."

"Oh, too bad," I said, trying to sound sincere even though I was grinning inside. "What about that secret weapon I heard about? I guess if Cokie's out, the secret weapon's gone, too."

"Oh, no," said Grace. "We still have that."

"You *do*?" I asked. I'd been so sure the secret weapon was all in Cokie's head.

"Yeah," said Grace. "It's Mari. Mari Drabek. Don't you know her dad's the dessert chef at Chez Maurice? He taught her everything he knows. She's been baking since she was five years old." Grace gave me a smug grin.

My face fell, and I couldn't think of a thing to say. "Um, well, good luck!" I finally squeaked out. Then I ran off to find Mary Anne and give her the bad news.

Fortunately, Mary Anne wasn't as worried as I was, and she calmed me down. But now, in my room with Shea, flipping through magazines in a desperate search for ideas with the contest only two days away, even Mary Anne was starting to lose her cool.

"Okay," I said finally, putting down the last

issue of *Chocolate Lover's*. "Let's not panic. After all, we don't have to worry about recipes for each day of the contest. All we have to do today is figure out one recipe, for the first day. If that one works out, we'll keep using it. If not, we'll try another."

That was the way the contest worked: it was up to the contestants to decide whether it was best to keep perfecting one recipe or to go on to others as the contest moved from the preliminaries, which would be held over the first three days, to the finals, when the five best teams or individuals would have one last chance to impress the judges. All we had to do for now was hang in through the preliminaries — and I thought I knew how to do it.

"I'm going to design a *great*-looking cake," I said firmly. "Something really fancy. I know it'll keep us in the contest."

"And I'll help figure out how to put it together," said Shea.

"Okay," said Mary Anne doubtfully. "You two work on that. But I'm going to try to find this old dessert recipe of my mother's. Something in this cookbook just reminded me of a recipe my dad used to tell me about, and I bet if I can figure it out it'll be a winner."

Mary Anne sounded sure of herself, and sort of mysterious. I decided she'd clue me

Saturday,

The Battle of the Bakers has begun!
And may the best man, woman, boy,
or girl win. (Especially if that person
happens to be a BSC member!) I have
a feeling this is going to be an exciting
contest. Meanwhile, things are pretty
exciting in the day care center, too.
How could they not be, with all those
kids? But we're having fun — right???
I think my main goal for the duration
of the contest will be to prevent Jackie R.
from causing Total Destruction.

"Jackie! Get down, please. NOW!"

Jackie Rodowsky (Shea's little brother) is a very cute, seven-year-old redhead who is known to the members of the BSC as the Walking Disaster. We adore him, but we're also *very* aware of the fact that wherever Jackie goes, chaos follows. He's totally accident-prone, and any breakable objects near him seem to have a habit of hurling themselves to the floor. Plus, he can't seem to resist climbing up, over, and on top of any structure he comes across. Which was what he was doing at that moment. Which was why Kristy was calling to him.

Jackie grinned down at Kristy from his perch on top of a long sofa that runs along the windowed wall of the faculty lounge at the high school. It was the first day of the baking contest, and also, of course, the first day of our day-care center. Almost every member of the BSC was there, except Jessi, who had to attend a special dance class, Shannon, who was shopping with her mom, and Dawn, who had a job sitting for Jenny Prezzioso, one of our regular clients.

It was a good thing the rest of us were at the day-care center. The room was full of kids. Jackie's four-year-old brother Archie was there, and so was Shea. Jamie and Lucy Newton were on hand, as well as some other regular clients of the BSC: Carolyn and Marilyn Arnold, who are eight-year-old identical twins, Charlotte Johanssen, and Hannie and Linny Papadakis. Hannie's a seven-year-old girl, and Linny's a nine-year-old boy, and they live in Kristy's neighborhood. Also, Kerry (Logan's sister) was there, just hanging out while she waited for the afternoon's under-sixteen baking contest to begin.

Plus, we found plenty of kids we didn't know, kids whose parents had come from out of town to compete in the Battle of the Bakers. It wasn't easy getting to know the new kids at once. The only reason I can even remember their names is that Mary Anne (awesome BSC secretary that she is) wrote down all their names and ages, plus a little bit about each kid. Here are her notes:

Emily Austen, age eight. Blonde, straight hair. Super-energetic. Loves to read, make up poems, and sing songs.

Tyler, age twelve. Emily's older brother. Doesn't really need a sitter, but decided to "hang out with the kids." Special note to Stacey: Tyler is diabetic. Special note to Kristy: Tyler loves baseball.

35

<u>Nichole Lavista</u>, age six.
Black curls, cute, full of tricks.
Note to Claud: loves to draw
and paint.

<u>Taylor</u> and <u>Tyler</u>, Nichole's
adorable three-year-old
twin brothers. Watch out!
These two are wild and will
make the biggest mess they
can as soon as your back
is turned.

<u>Morgan Singer</u>, age eight.
Light brown straight hair,
serious face. Smart and
full of fun. Came all the
way from New York City,
along with

<u>Dana</u>, Morgan's baby sister.

<u>Kyle Farmer</u>, nine. Black
wavy hair, blue eyes (he'll
break a lot of hearts someday!)
Outgoing, makes friends
easily.

<u>Megan</u>, Kyle's seven-year-
old sister. Same coloring, but
different personality. Very
quiet — and I really hate to
say it, but kind of <u>sneaky</u>.

As you can probably imagine, the scene in that faculty lounge was wild. There were twenty kids, ranging in age from a few months to twelve years old, plus six baby-sitters, all packed into a room that really wasn't all that big to begin with. Not only that, but it was crowded with stuff Marty had rounded up for us: napping mats, easels and art supplies, kid-sized tables and chairs, giant blocks, piles of books, and other day-care necessities. Not to mention that we'd all brought our Kid-Kits.

The place was like a three-ring circus, and Kristy was the ringmaster. It's amazing how that kind of chaos really brings out the best in her. What may seem like bossiness at other times comes across as excellent leadership. Her big mouth becomes an asset (she was the only one of us who could make herself heard), and her need to organize (which I think she overdoes sometimes) is a lifesaver.

We had arrived early, at seven-thirty. By eight, kids were already trickling in, and by nine we were at full capacity, and you could no longer hear yourself think. Kids were running around the room screaming. Babies were crying. Blocks were being tossed. Tyler the twelve-year-old was trying to hide away in a corner. Tyler the three-year-old was throwing red paint at his twin brother. And Jackie Rodowsky, the Walking Disaster, was doing his version of a tightrope act, walking across the back of that sofa, holding on to the window drapes for balance.

That's when Kristy took charge.

"Jackie! Get down, please. *Now!*" She stood with her hands on her hips and waited until he climbed down off the couch, looking sheepish. We BSC members gathered nearby, waiting to hear what would come next. "Okay," said Kristy, once Jackie was safely down, "what we have to do here is to create some order. First, let's divide up the kids by age, so each group can be involved in some activity that's right for their level." She turned to me. "Claud, why don't you take the threes and fours" — she gestured toward Jamie, Taylor, Tyler, and Archie — "over by the blocks."

She turned to Mary Anne, who was holding a crying Lucy. "It sounds like Lucy may need changing," she said to Mary Anne. "How about if you take her and Dana over by the changing table? We can make that the baby area."

"I'll help watch Dana while you change Lucy," Logan volunteered, smiling at Mary Anne.

"Good." Kristy nodded. "But when Lucy's all set, we'll need you to help with the older kids. I bet some of them would love to play outside for a while."

"So would I!" yelled Jackie, who was the only kid listening to our quick organizational meeting.

"Okay," Kristy agreed. "How about if Logan and I go outside with anyone who wants to come? Stacey and Mal can stay inside with the rest of the older kids."

"Deal," said Jackie.

We all laughed. "Deal," I said, echoing Jackie. Then I ran off to catch Taylor, who was hefting a giant block over his brother's head.

Once we'd divided the kids up, the situation became a lot more manageable. The room was quieter after Kristy and Logan took a bunch of kids outside, even though Linny, Morgan, Carolyn, Kerry, and Charlotte quickly became involved in a game of "restaurant." I couldn't pay too much attention to their game, because my four young charges kept me busy. Taylor and Tyler soon pulled Archie and Jamie into a wild game I thought of as Construction and Demolition: over and over again, they built the highest buildings they could out of the blocks and then, shrieking with delight, knocked them down. It wasn't the quietest activity, but it kept them occupied.

After about an hour, Kristy and Logan came back inside with the other kids, who immediately joined the restaurant game. The kids,

Kristy noticed, were pretending to be cooks and waiters and waitresses.

"I think they feel left out of the baking contest," Kristy said to Mary Anne, who had put the babies down for naps — Dana in a porta-crib and Lucy in her car seat, which her mom had brought in.

"Too bad there isn't an actual kitchen in here," Mary Anne said, nodding toward a counter with a sink, a mini-fridge, a micro-wave, and a coffee-maker, which were all the faculty lounge really needed. "If there was, the kids could do some supervised cooking, and maybe play restaurant for real."

"That's it!" said Kristy.

"What?" asked Mary Anne, bewildered.

"What if we let them practice some 'cooking' right here. Then, on the last day of the contest, they can open a pretend restaurant? The parents will love it!"

"But what kind of cooking can they do?" asked Mary Anne.

"Oh, they can make lots of things," Kristy said. "Anything that doesn't need cooking. We can ask the parents to donate some money toward food. It'll be great! Trust me."

Just then, Logan approached Kristy. "I think we have a problem," he told her in a low voice.

"What is it?" she asked.

"Kyle says there was a calculator sitting on

the table before, when everybody first arrived. Now the kids want to use it for their game, and it's not there anymore. He says he thinks somebody must have taken it."

Kristy frowned. "I would hate to think that was true," she said. "How about if we do a quiet search for it, before we start accusing the kids of stealing?"

The word went around to all the BSC members, and we started to look for the calculator. I searched my corner, wondering if one of my charges had picked it up, but it was nowhere in sight. Mary Anne checked behind the changing table, but it wasn't there. Stacey and Kristy hunted through the cupboards and found plenty of nondairy creamer and red pencils (important teacher supplies, I guess), but no calculator.

Finally, as Kristy told us later, Kyle cornered her while she was alone near the sink and told her that he'd seen Megan take the calculator. "It's in her backpack," he said, and when Kristy called Megan to her and asked her to open up her backpack, it turned out that Kyle was right. Kristy was shocked.

"Don't tell our mom," Kyle begged. "She always gets so mad when Megan takes things."

Kristy turned to Megan. "I won't tell this time," she said. "But I'm putting you on warning. If you're not on your best behavior, I'm going to have to take action. Understand?"

Megan nodded and shrugged. She had, Kristy told us later, this strangely blank look on her face.

"She didn't deny taking the calculator," Kristy said wonderingly. "But she didn't seem to feel or act guilty about doing it, the way most kids would if they were caught. We'll have to keep our eyes on her."

That was why Mary Anne mentioned — reluctantly — Megan's "sneaky" behavior in her notes. None of us wanted to believe that we had a problem kid in our group. Besides, even though the scene in the faculty lounge was chaotic, we could tell it was going to be a lot of fun, especially with Jackie Rodowsky providing extra entertainment.

CHAPTER 5

"Yikes!" Mary Anne said. We were in the midst of trying to tidy up the faculty lounge while the kids, who had eaten the lunches they'd brought, had "quiet time."

"What?" I asked. I put down a pile of books.

"Check out the time," she answered, sticking out her wrist so I could see her watch. "The adult contest is about to end."

"Yikes!" I echoed. "That means the parents will be here soon to pick up their kids. And it's almost time for *us* to start baking." Suddenly, I felt butterflies in my stomach.

"Claud?" Mary Anne asked in a shaky voice.

"Yes?"

"Are you nervous?"

"Me? Nervous? Ha-ha-ha," I laughed. "Don't be silly. This contest is no big deal. We could win it with our eyes closed." I hoped I sounded confident. If Mary Anne went all ner-

43

vous on me, I didn't know *what* to do. I could control my own butterflies, but if I had to take care of somebody else's flock, too, I knew I'd be in trouble.

Mary Anne smiled. "You're right," she said in a stronger voice.

"Ready to go?" I asked her. I grabbed my backpack, pulled out my latest creation, and stuck it on my head. "What do you think?"

Mary Anne burst out laughing. "It's great!" she said. "I love it. Will you make me one?"

I took the hat off and examined it. "It is pretty great, isn't it?" I said. The day before, my dad had driven me to a restaurant supply store on the outskirts of town, and I'd bought one of those big, white, puffy chef's hats. Then, back at home, I'd gone to work with my fabric paints. The result? A stunning Kishi creation (if I do say so myself). The hat was covered with baking images. Brightly colored rolling pins, cake pans, mixing bowls, and measuring spoons danced all over it.

Mary Anne reached into her own backpack, pulled out a frilly white apron, and tied it on. "This was my mother's," she said shyly. "I found it in a trunk in the attic. My grandmother once told me that she made it for my mom when she — my mom — was my age."

"It looks great," I said. "And I bet it'll bring us good luck."

44

"Not that we need it!" said Shea, from behind us. "Our team *rules*!" We gave each other high-fives.

"Remember, though," said Kristy, who had just joined us. "No dirty tricks, or the Cake Cops will be on your case." She was wearing a red baseball cap with a white "C" on it.

"Nice hat," said Shea.

"I'm not really a Cincinnati Reds fan," she answered, taking it off and examining it. But I thought the 'C' would be a good symbol for Cake Cop. I'm supposed to be sort of undercover, so act like you don't know me, okay?"

"Right," I said. Then I noticed that parents were coming to pick up their kids, and that Austin had come to meet Logan and Kerry. It was time to head for the kitchens.

Stacey and Mal, who were staying behind to watch the few kids who would be there through the afternoon, wished us luck. "Remember, it's just a preliminary round today," said Mal. She must have noticed that we looked a little nervous.

When we arrived in the gym, I suddenly became a *lot* nervous. It seemed like zillions of kids were milling around. There were only ten teams in the junior division, but considering that every team consisted of two or three people, that made for a lot of kids.

I exchanged glances with Mary Anne, and I had a feeling I looked as scared to her as she did to me. But then I shook off my nerves. "Come on," I said to her, and to the rest of my friends. "Let's scope out the situation."

We walked around for a few minutes, but then, suddenly, Marty's voice came over the loudspeaker. "All team members please report to your work areas immediately," he said. "The Mrs. Goode's Cookware Battle of the Bakers, junior division, is about to begin with today's preliminary round."

Mary Anne, Shea, and I scrambled to find our workstation. Earlier, when we'd dropped off our baking supplies, we had found out which stove we would be using. But now, in the mad rush, it wasn't so easy to locate. "Whew," Mary Anne said, when she saw the two bulging grocery bags we'd set on the counter. "We'd better start unpacking." She reached into one of the bags.

I looked around, still trying to check out the other teams. I knew there was no way I'd learn everybody's name that day. Fortunately, Kristy was in the perfect position to check out the contestants. She even took notes on every team, identifying them by their station numbers, and gave them to me later on. Here's what she wrote down:

46

Team One: (Barf!) Cokie, Grace, and Mari. (Except that Cokie is out. So it's just Grace and Ms.-Secret-Weapon Mari.)

Team Two: (Out-of-towners) Julie Liu, Sinai Choi, Celeste Baskett. Julie looks a little older than most kids here — she must be almost sixteen. And I think she and Sinai, who looks about thirteen, are cousins.

Team Three: Pete Black, Erica Blumberg, and Lauren Hoffman. Another SMS team, probably not a team to worry about.

Team Four: Bill Korman, who lives across the street from me, and two of his friends from Stoneybrook Day School, Greg Wilson and David Simpson. They're all nine, and they seem like smart kids.

Team Five: (Out-of-towners) Rachel Kleinman, Anna Atamian. These two look as if they know what they're doing. I think they're both around fourteen.

Team Six: (Out-of-towners) Joey Casella and Mickey Stone. Both probably about fourteen. Note to Claud and Stacey: Cute Boy Alert! I think this team may be a wild card.

<u>Team Seven</u>: Mary Anne, Shea, and Claudia. Go, team!

<u>Team Eight</u>: Logan, Kerry, and Austin. Ditto!

<u>Team Nine</u>: Sara Hill (she's nine) and two of her friends who aren't BSC clients, Elizabeth Sayers and Brittany DePew.

And finally, (ta - daaa!),

<u>Team Ten</u>: (O-O-T) Diane McVie, Tiffany Sweet, and Jennifer Downey. (Jennifer is also known as "Precious." Could you hurl? I heard her mother call her that.) They're probably fifteen, but I bet they could pass for thirty. This team wins the prize for most makeup and longest fingernails. I don't think they're serious about their baking.

Mary Anne, Shea, and I were working at station seven, between Logan's team and the Cute Boy team, across from Julie Liu's team, and kitty-corner to Grace's and Mari's team.

Since the stations were all pretty close together, and the dividers weren't high, it wasn't much of a stretch to see and hear what was happening around us. And what went on during that afternoon was nothing short of total insanity. The hours passed like minutes, from the time Marty said "Ready, bakers? Then . . . *go!*" and set the timer, to the time a bell went off and we had to stop baking.

The end result for my team? The beautiful cake I'd planned came out of the oven looking flatter than a pancake. But you know what? It wasn't my fault. Neither was the burnt-to-a-crisp cake that Logan's team came up with. I didn't want to believe it at first, but when we looked at the evidence later, it was all too clear. There were dirty doings at the Battle of the Bakers.

But I'm getting ahead of myself. I should explain what happened, and try to give you an idea of what the atmosphere in that gym was like for those crazy hours that Saturday afternoon.

"How's it going, Team Seven?"

That was Marty, stopping by to check up on us, soon after we'd gotten started. I smiled at him. "We're just fine," I said. I was proud of how neat our station looked. My banana-walnut fudge ripple cake called for a lot of ingredients, but Mary Anne, Shea, and I had lined them all up carefully. We were organized, unlike Grace and Mari. I couldn't help noticing that Mari seemed to be tossing ingredients around rather carelessly. I had to wonder how she could possibly live up to Cokie's bragging.

Logan's team, on the other hand, seemed to be taking things very, very seriously. Like us, they had lined up their ingredients carefully, but I also noticed Logan making marks on some kind of checklist as they began to bake. Now that seemed a little *too* organized!

"One of those boys on Team Four says he knows you," Marty said, gesturing toward Bill Korman.

"Oh, sure," I said. "We know most of the Stoneybrook contestants."

"Team Six asked me to introduce you later on, when you have time," Marty mentioned, with a grin. I blushed. Team Six was the Cute Boy team. Just then, someone called to Marty and he looked around. "Be right there, Julie," he answered. "She needs a hand figuring out that stove, I think," he told us. Then he was off, and we went back to work.

It wasn't easy, baking in those little cubicles. Especially since there were no sinks. People were constantly running back and forth to sinks in the locker room, carrying dirty bowls and spoons or measuring cups full of water that they needed for their recipes. Now, I don't remember this happening, but at one point, I guess Mary Anne, Shea, and I all must have been away from our station, on the way to or from the locker room, at the same time. Same with Logan's team.

How do I know? Because at one point during that afternoon, *somebody* substituted flour for our baking soda. I didn't find out until after I'd used the "baking soda," which is why our cake fell flat. By the time I figured it out, all I could find on the baking soda box was one smudged, floury fingerprint. And *somebody* changed the settings on Logan's team's oven, turning it up high and changing the baking time from twenty-five to forty-five minutes. They didn't leave any fingerprints at all at his station.

Somebody who? Well, let's put it this way. Grace and Mari, whose station was near ours, had no trouble at all. In fact, their sticky buns won that day's prize. Hmmm.

I'm not saying that they were the guilty party. But it was awfully easy to imagine Cokie putting them up to no good. Still, some other strange things went on that afternoon. For example, Stacey told me later that Jackie Rodowsky, who had stayed at the day-care center during the afternoon session, disappeared for a while and came back with flour all over his shirt. But we knew *he* wouldn't sabotage our contest entries. Would he?

And Kristy told us she'd had to help Marty escort more than one parent out of the contest area. Jennifer "Precious" Downey's mom had been hovering around her station. And Rachel Kleinman's dad kept popping up throughout the afternoon.

Who had done the dirty work? So far, it was hard to tell. But one thing was clear: somebody obviously cared a little too much about winning that contest. And I sure hoped I could find out who — before the culprit ruined my chances.

CHAPTER 6

"Okay, Shea," I said. "I'm ready for that teaspoon of vanilla." As Shea measured out what I needed, I glanced up and caught Grace glaring at me across the dividers. I stared back at her.

"I didn't do it," I called. "I swear, I didn't do it."

She just gave me this look that said "yeah, sure," and went back to her baking.

It was Sunday, the second day of the Battle of the Bakers. And Team Seven was running behind. We were working on a new recipe I'd come up with, for a seven-layer mocha-strawberry cake (Mary Anne still hadn't found her mother's recipe), and I was becoming very worried about whether we'd finish on time. The cake should already have been in the oven, so I could be blending exactly the right colors for the icing, which was going to be dusty-rose with lilac contrasts. The cake would be gorgeous — if we ever finished it.

Fortunately, everybody else was running late, too. And when I tell you why, you'll know why Grace was glaring at me.

It had happened soon after we started baking that day. Grace and Mari must have whipped up their recipe in no time flat, and shoved it right into the oven. I nudged Mary Anne when I noticed Grace setting the timer. "They're in a hurry, aren't they?" I whispered. "I think Mari rushes things, know what I mean?"

Mary Anne nodded, then we turned back to measuring and sifting. We had arrived at our station early that day, although we hadn't beaten Marty, Julie, Rachel, or Anne to the gym. (They must have shown up super early.) We set up our ingredients carefully again, and agreed that we would do our best not to leave our workstation unwatched. Nobody was going to sabotage our recipe that day. We needed to make a good impression on the judges, and time was running out.

Anyway, there we were, following each step carefully. Shea had just turned on the oven to preheat it, when I first smelled smoke. "Shea!" I said, "is that *our* oven smoking?"

He opened the oven door, bent down, and gave a big sniff. "Nope," he said, shaking his head. "At least, I don't think so."

"Well, something's burning!" said Mary Anne. She put down the eggbeater she had been using and looked around. A few other heads popped up over nearby dividers, and I heard people asking each other what was burning. We were all sniffing and peering around, when suddenly I heard Grace shriek.

"Fire!" she screamed. "Oh! Oh! Oh! Fire!" She was hopping around, waving her hands frantically. "Help!" she yelled.

Mari looked calmer, at least until black smoke began to trickle out of the oven. "My *cake!*" she said, when she saw that. She bent to open the oven door, but slammed it shut immediately when billows of smoke poured out. Then she joined Grace's cries of "Fire! Fire!"

I saw Marty run toward them, looking around frantically as if he were trying to locate somebody — or something.

One of the people in the gym (I don't know who) finally had the presence of mind to pull the fire alarm, and hearing its loud clanging made us all move fast. Within minutes, the gym was empty (except for the firefighters, who had shown up almost immediately), and the contestants, contest organizers, and judges were standing in the parking lot outside.

The firefighters had the situation under control in no time, and soon they let us return to the gym. We clustered around Grace's and Mari's workstation to hear what the fire marshall had to say.

"Is my cake all right?" asked Mari, pushing her way to the front of the crowd.

"Afraid not, miss," he said. "Looks like you put a little too much of something in there. That batter bubbled up all over the place, and poured out of its pan. When it hit the burners, it ignited."

"Too much baking powder," somebody muttered.

Mari whirled around. "There wasn't any baking powder!" she said. "The recipe doesn't call for any."

"Guess some went in there by mistake," said the fire marshall, with a shrug. "You'll be able to use your oven again now, but I don't think that cake'll taste too good."

Mari looked at Grace. "Did you put any baking powder in the batter?" she asked.

Grace turned bright red and shook her head. "No," she said.

"Baking *soda*?" asked Mari.

"No!" said Grace, turning even redder. "I only did what you told me to do."

I almost felt bad for her. It couldn't have been fun to be interrogated in front of that crowd of people. (Nobody had gone back to their stations yet.) "Practically all I did was sift the flour and mix that cornstarch with a little orange juice, just like you said," said Grace, pointing to a box of cornstarch on their counter.

Mari looked puzzled for a second. Then, as if a light bulb had gone on over her head, she grabbed the cornstarch box, stuck two fingers into its opening, and took out a pinch. She tasted it. "Ha!" she shouted. "That's not cornstarch. That's baking soda. Somebody switched it on us!" She looked triumphant, and Grace looked relieved.

"I knew it wasn't my fault," she whispered.

"Now, now," said one of the judges, a skinny man who writes a restaurant review column for the *Stoneybrook News*. "Of course it wasn't your fault. It wasn't anybody's fault. Just a little mistake, that's all. Let's not go jumping to conclusions."

"That's right," said another judge, a woman who manages a fancy restaurant in Stamford, called Maria's. "After all, why would anyone ruin your recipe on purpose?"

Mari looked as if she were about to answer that question, but Marty Nisson jumped in and cut her off. "Right!" he said enthusiastically. "We're all friends here. We should just be happy that nobody was hurt. And I'm sure the judges will agree to give you an extension on your baking time today, since you've had a problem. I know the Mrs. Goode's Cookware Company would want it that way."

The judges all agreed, and after Mari and Grace thanked them, everybody went back to work. That's when I noticed Mari and Grace whispering to each other and then glaring at Mary Anne and me. Just because we've never exactly been friends with their friend, Cokie, they thought we would sabotage their cake. Can you believe it?

(Of course, I had suspected *them* — or Cokie — the day before. But that was different.)

I decided to ignore their stares and go on with my baking. After all, I had a contest to win. But the fire wasn't the only distraction that afternoon.

First of all, Stacey popped up at our workstation while Mary Anne and I were trying to transfer three beaten eggs and a half cup of milk from one bowl into another. "Did you see Jackie in here a while ago?" she asked.

"I didn't," said Shea, who was standing by with some paper towels.

"Me, neither," said Mary Anne and I.

"Well, he left the day-care room again," Stacey said. "And when he came back, he had flour — or something white and powdery — all over his shirt. Again!"

Mary Anne and I exchanged glances, raised

our eyebrows, and then shook our heads. Something white and powdery, such as baking soda? Why would Jackie want to mess up Grace's and Mari's cake? But there was no time to tell Stacey what had happened, or to talk about what else Jackie might have been up to. If we didn't put our cake into the oven within about two minutes, we'd never finish on time.

Soon after Stacey left, and right after I did finally put the cake into the oven, I saw Kristy escorting Rachel's father to the door of the gym. She stopped by our workstation on her way back. "He was hanging around talking to Rachel and Anna," she explained. "Checking up on their ingredients and stuff. I had to ask him to leave." She shrugged. "Just another day in the life of a Cake Cop," she added, grinning.

Just then we both heard angry voices from the station across the way. "Don't you *care*?" asked a woman. "Where's your enthusiasm?"

"Forget about enthusiasm," said a man. "Where's your creativity? Your sense of design?"

Kristy and I looked up to see a man and a woman standing on either side of Julie Liu. They looked angry, and Julie looked as if she'd rather be anywhere else but between the two of them. Kristy looked back at me, mouthed "see you!" and took off in their direction.

Later, I found out that the couple are Julie's parents. (Kristy needed Marty's help to escort them out.) They are instructors at a cooking school in Stamford, and they have very high expectations for Julie. Kristy had the feeling that they wanted her to win the Battle of the Bakers because they'd gain publicity for their business. Can you imagine? Poor Julie. Watching her that day, I could tell she was under a lot of pressure — and that she wasn't having any fun. Her teammates, Sinai and Celeste, kept trying to cheer her up, but she seemed unhappy and distracted.

Distracted, like me. I'll admit it. With all that was going on in the gym, I was having a hard time paying attention to my baking that day. But the good news was that by looking at the cake my team came up with at the end of the afternoon, you never would have known. It was beautiful, and all the judges said so.

But there was also bad news.

The cake *tasted* unbelievably awful. Sort of like rubber. With glue icing.

I saw one of the judges run for the locker room after she took a bite.

Mary Anne and Shea tried to cheer me up. "It really was pretty," said Shea loyally.

"You mixed that pink color just right," Mary Anne added.

Meanwhile, we watched as the judges

checked out the other contestants' efforts. Rachel's and Anna's apricot upside-down cake looked great, and so did Julie's team's chocolate angel-food cake, although I heard one of the judges say it was "a bit too simple." Mari and Grace never did finish their entry, even with the extension they were given.

But guess who won the day's prize? Logan, Kerry, and Austin! They had come up with a new variation on a fruitcake recipe, adding pecans and dried currants, and the judges went crazy for it.

I was happy for them, but also a little jealous, and disappointed that my own cake hadn't turned out well. I knew Shea and Mary Anne felt the same way. But at least, I told myself, there hadn't been any more sabotage after the fire. Maybe the Battle of the Bakers would be a fair fight from now on.

CHAPTER 7

"Mary Anne! Hi! Can you hear me?" It was Tuesday evening, and I was standing on the patio in my backyard.

"Of course I can," said Mary Anne. "Why?"

"I'm trying out this cool new cordless phone my dad just brought home," I said. "Wait a second." I walked farther away from the house. "Can you hear me now?" I asked. I loved the feeling of being able to roam around while I was on the phone. I get tired of staring at the same old stuff while I talk.

"I can hear you," said Mary Anne, "but you're a little fuzzy."

"Oh, okay," I said. "I must be moving out of range." By that time I was so far away from the house that I was practically in our neighbor's yard. I walked back toward the house. "Better?"

"Much."

"Cool," I said. By then I was near the barbecue grill. "I could be out here flipping burgers, talking on the phone at the same time." I grabbed a barbecue tool and pretended to turn over a few hamburgers.

"That's great, Claud," said Mary Anne. "But listen — "

"I could even go back into the kitchen for a package of hot dogs," I interrupted her, talking as I walked to the sliding door, opened it, and entered the kitchen, "and then go back out and toss them on the grill." I was on the patio again. The cordless phone was going to change my life. I could see it already.

"Claudia," said Mary Anne, "I'm glad you like your new phone, but — but we really have to talk."

"We *are* talking," I said, confused.

"I mean about the Battle of the Bakers," said Mary Anne.

"About the sabotage and everything? We talked about that at yesterday's BSC meeting, and I thought we agreed that we'd do our best to figure out who was behind it."

"Right," said Mary Anne. "We did. But there's — there's something else we need to discuss."

"So we'll talk about it at tomorrow's meeting. Kristy the Cake Cop won't mind. Or are you saying that we need to have an emergency meeting?" I didn't understand what she was hinting at.

"No," said Mary Anne, sounding a little exasperated. I heard her sigh. "What I'm saying is that there's something you and I need to discuss. Just the two of us."

"Oh! Why didn't you say so?"

"I've been trying to," she answered. "It's just that, well, I really wouldn't want to hurt your feelings, Claud, but — but — "

"But my recipes aren't cutting it, and if we don't do something, we're never going to make the finals. Right?" I was smiling. I stood up and started to stroll around the outside of the house, still enjoying that cordless feeling.

Mary Anne was speechless for a second.

"It's okay," I reassured her. "I'm an artist, not a chef. I know my cakes have been awful." I giggled. "Wait. I take it back. They haven't been awful, they've been disgusting. Inedible. Mondo-horrendous. Barf-o-rama. Puke-tacular.

"But beautiful," Mary Anne added, in a timid voice. "They really have been gorgeous cakes, Claud." Then she started to laugh. "Puke-tacular?" she asked. "What kind of word is that?"

"I made it up," I said, proudly. "It's, like, puke plus spectacular. Like it?"

"I love it," she said. "And I would love your cakes, too, if they only tasted as good as they looked."

"But they don't," I said.

"No, they don't. I'm sorry, Claud, but they just don't. Shea agrees, but he's too shy to say so."

"I know," I said. "So what do we do?" By that time, I had walked around the outside of the house twice, and I was ready to sit down. I headed back inside and made myself comfortable on the couch.

"I want to try again to find that recipe my mother used to make," Mary Anne was saying, "and I could use your help."

"No problem," I said. "But why this certain recipe?"

"Remember back when my dad would hardly ever talk about my mom?" Mary Anne asked. "Well, even then, the one thing he *did* talk about was her chocolate-cherry cake. He raved about it. He'd tell me how she used to make it for his birthday every year, and also on special occasions, or if he asked her nicely. Supposedly, it was the best cake in the world. Moist, chocolate-y, delicious."

"Not puke-tacular at all, I guess," I said.

"Not a bit puke-tacular, according to my dad. I can't tell you more than that, though, since I never tasted it."

"So how are we going to find the recipe?" I asked.

"I thought we could start by rummaging around in the attic," she answered. "When Dad and I moved in with Sharon and Dawn, we brought all the boxes that used to be in our attic. Maybe there's an old recipe book in one of them."

"Let's do it first thing tomorrow!" I said. I was excited. For one thing, I love mysteries, and this was beginning to sound like one. For another, I also happen to love poking around in old attics. You never know what you'll find.

And that's how Mary Anne and I ended up inside a dusty, hot attic on one of the most beautiful days of the summer. We had invited Shea, but he had a piano lesson. It was just me, Mary Anne, and about three tons of boxes. No cordless phone. No junk food. We went right to work, since there was nothing else to do.

We opened box after box. Some of them were filled with winter clothes, and seeing those mittens and scarves made me feel even hotter. Others were stuffed with canceled checks and tax records. *Bor*ing! And one was full of Mary Anne's old little-girl dresses — not the ones from when she was *really* little, but the ones from seventh grade, when her dad was still treating her as if she were eight years old.

"Look at this one!" I said, holding up a plaid jumper. "This is actually almost fashionable again, now that the schoolgirl look is in." I laughed, expecting Mary Anne to join me, but she was silent. "Mary Anne?" I asked. "What's the matter? I didn't mean to make fun of your dress."

She sniffed. "I know," she said. "It's not the dress. It's these letters." She showed me the box she was looking through, which was marked "correspondence." "These are the letters between my dad and my grandmother. The ones that upset me so much when I first discovered them."

I winced, remembering. "That was awful," I said. "You thought your dad had given you away when you were a baby."

"He didn't, though," said Mary Anne. "He just sent me to my grandparents for a little while, after my mom died. He was having trouble coping with his grief *and* a baby."

"But then your grandparents wanted to keep you, right?"

"Uh-huh. So my dad had to argue with them a little. Finally they agreed to let me come back, but then they didn't want to see me again because they thought it would be too painful. That's why I didn't even know I had grandparents until after my grandfather died and my grandmother made contact again."

"You're pretty close to her now, aren't you?" I asked, reaching out to give Mary Anne a hug. She was still sniffling a little.

She nodded. "That first trip out to Iowa was scary," she said. "But now I love her, and we talk pretty often. She tells me lots of stuff about my mom. You know, how her name was Alma, but her pet name was Sweetie-Pie, and how she looked just like me as a girl, and what kinds of things she used to do. . . ."

"That's it!" I said. "I bet *she* knows the recipe. Maybe your grandmother's even the one who taught your mom how to make that cake. Come on, let's leave this stuffy attic and make a phone call."

We thumped down the stairs.

Mary Anne found her grandmother's number and dialed it without wasting another second. I watched as she stood listening to the phone on the other end ring and ring. She started to look disappointed as she realized that nobody was home. Then, suddenly, her eyes lit up, but just for a second. She covered the mouthpiece of the phone. "I thought it was her," she said. "But it's just her answering machine."

"Leave a message!" I said.

Mary Anne listened for the beep. "Hi, Grandma," she said, when she'd heard it. "It's me, Mary Anne. How are you? I'm fine."

I rolled my hands in that "move it along" motion.

Mary Anne started to talk faster. "I'm calling because I need your help. I'm trying to find this recipe of my mother's, and I thought you might know something about it. It's for a baking contest, and I need it this weekend. So please, *please* call me if you hear this message, okay? 'Bye! I love you!"

She hung up. "I think we're out of luck," she said. She had this hopeless look on her face.

"Why? You left a message. She'll call back, won't she?"

"I just remembered that the last time we talked she told me she was going away for a couple of weeks, to visit an old friend," Mary Anne said. "She may not even hear that message until after the contest is over."

"Oh, well," I said, giving her a hug. I hate to see Mary Anne unhappy. "At least you tried."

By then, it was almost time for our BSC meeting, so we headed to my house, talking over other recipe possibilities as we walked. We'd narrowed it down to a fudge ripple cake or a raspberry double-walnut coffee cake by the time we arrived in my room. The other BSC members were already there.

And, as it turned out, they were talking about the Battle of the Bakers. It seemed to be the only thing on everybody's mind. For one thing, we were working hard on our day-care kids' "restaurant," to be held on the last day of the contest. But even more important, everybody was thinking over the sabotage and wondering about possible suspects. (I'm not the only one in the BSC who loves mysteries. We all adore them. And we've solved more than a couple!)

I mentioned Grace again, but then I asked if anyone else had come up with a suspect.

"I've been thinking it over," Kristy said. "Mr. Kleinman sure has been making me suspicious. He's always hanging around, checking up on what his daughter's doing."

"So?" I asked. "So are Julie Liu's parents."

"That's true," said Kristy. "But I think it's just that they'd really like her to win. They don't seem to *skulk* around the way Mr. Kleinman does. Anyway, I was so suspicious of him that I made a few calls, and guess what I found out?"

We leaned forward.

"He used to work for Mrs. Goode's Cookware!" said Kristy triumphantly.

"Uh-huh," said Stacey. "That's interesting, but not *that* interesting."

"It is when you know that he left because he was fired," said Kristy. "I bet anything he's what they call a 'disgruntled ex-employee.' He might do anything to see his daughter win and 'show up' the company."

We nodded thoughtfully, and then my clock switched over to five-thirty and Kristy called the meeting to order. "Let's just keep an eye on Mr. Kleinman, okay? And on Grace, too, of course. Now, on to club business," she said. "Should we plan our grocery shopping for the weekend? We want to make sure we have plenty of food on hand for our 'restaurant.' "

After that, the meeting sped by. There was so much to think about and do for the day-care center that for a little while I almost forgot about the sabotage. Almost — but not quite. I wouldn't really be able to put it out of my mind until I knew I'd done everything I could to solve the mystery.

CHAPTER 8

"Are you finding everything you need, miss?"

I turned around and saw a smiling, bald-headed clerk wearing a green apron.

"Just about," I answered. I checked the list in my hand. "Let's see. I have the forty-watt lightbulb, the strapping tape, and the rubber plug for the bathroom sink. I guess all I'm missing is the ant poison."

"Right this way," said the man, leading me down an aisle.

I was at the hardware store in Stoneybrook. It was Friday, the day before the final weekend of the Battle of the Bakers. Since I didn't have a sitting job that morning, my mom had asked me to run a few errands in town. I love shopping anytime, anywhere — even at hardware stores, so I didn't mind.

"Here we go, miss," said the clerk, showing

me the shelf where three different types of ant poison were displayed.

"Which one is the strongest?" I asked. We had a big ant problem in the garage, and my mom was worried that they were going to start finding their way into the kitchen if we didn't take care of them now.

"People have had good luck with this one," said the clerk, pointing to a brand packaged in a bright red box.

"It looks deadly," I said.

"Oh, it is," replied the clerk, with a chuckle. "All set, now? I'll ring you up." He headed toward the cash register, and I followed him.

Suddenly, I had the strange feeling that somebody was following *me*. I looked behind me, but I didn't see anybody, so I kept on walking.

"I heard that," somebody hissed in my ear.

I jumped in surprise, turned, and found Grace standing next to me.

"Hi, Grace," I said.

"Don't 'hi Grace' me," she said.

"Huh?" I didn't know what she was talking about.

"I heard that whole conversation," she said knowingly.

"Conversation?"

"About the ant poison. So tell me, whose

cake are you going to put it in?"

"Are you crazy?" I asked. "I'm not putting ant poison in anybody's cake! It's for our garage."

"Sure, sure," said Grace. "All the same, I think I'll warn the judges. This goes beyond sabotage. Somebody would really be sick if they ate ant poison, you know."

I shook my head. This was too much. By this time, the clerk who had helped me was already at the cash register, ringing up my stuff. I ran to him, paid him, and thanked him for helping me. When I turned to leave, Grace was still standing there. "I can't believe you think I would poison somebody's cake," I told her.

"Well, I wouldn't have believed you would stoop as low as you did last Saturday," she answered, "but you did, just to win some stupid cooking contest. You were the one who switched my cornstarch with baking soda, and you almost burned down the whole high school!"

"I didn't!" I cried. We had walked out of the store while we were arguing, and now we were standing on the sidewalk. "You're just accusing me because *you're* the one who messed up *my* cake on Saturday."

"What?" she asked. "I never went near your station."

Grace was staring me right in the eye as she said that, and when I saw the look on her face I knew she was telling the truth. "You didn't, did you," I said.

"Nope."

"Well, I didn't go near yours, either. And this," I held up the hardware-store bag, "really is for the ants in the garage."

"But if it wasn't you . . ." she began.

"And it wasn't you . . ." I said.

"Who was it?" we asked together.

Then, without saying a word, we walked to a bench together and sat down. Grace gave a half smile. "Sorry," she said.

"I'm sorry, too," I said. Then we both started to talk at once.

"Let's work on this together!" Grace said.

"Whoever's doing it doesn't want either of us to win," I pointed out.

"We need to make a list of clues," said Grace.

"And a list of suspects."

"Just like Nancy Drew," said Grace. "I love those books."

"You *do*?" I asked. "So do I." I grinned. I was finding out something interesting. Grace Blume could be a pretty decent person, once you took her away from Cokie. And it looked as if she might be a pretty decent detective, too.

We sat on that bench and talked for awhile. I filled her in on everything the BSC had discussed, including our suspicions about Mr. Kleinman. Soon, though, I realized that it might be a good idea to talk in a more private setting. "Hey, want to come over to my house?" I asked. "Or do you have other stuff to do?"

"No, I was just picking up some batteries for my Walkman," said Grace. "I can come."

I know Mary Anne and Dawn were surprised when I called and asked them to come over and help Grace and me with our detective work.

"Grace?" Mary Anne asked.

"Grace *Blume*?" Dawn said. She was on the extension.

"Right," I said impatiently. "I'll explain later. Just come on over. And if anyone else is free, can you call them?"

Soon we were gathered in my room: Grace and I, Mary Anne and Dawn, Kristy, and Jessi. (Mal was sitting for her sisters, and Stacey was sitting for Charlotte Johanssen.) I passed around some snacks I had rustled up from under my bed (Fritos), in my sock drawer (M&M's), and behind the dictionary on my desk (Twizzlers). I had also found an unused notebook, and I was taking notes as we munched away and talked over what was happening at the baking contest, why it was happening, and who might be responsible.

First, we tried to remember all the details of the crimes. Mary Anne and I figured out that whoever had sabotaged our cake on Saturday must have watched us closely and gone to our station when everybody on our team was away from it. There was only one time that had happened: Mary Anne was washing out a bowl in the locker room, Shea was fetching some water, and I was (I admit it) kind of flirting with the Cute Boy team at the next station. (I didn't mean to flirt. It just happened that I needed a clean dishtowel, and they had one. Mickey Stone, the blond boy, has the *sweetest* smile.)

Anyway, that's when whoever it was must have switched flour for our baking soda. And the only evidence left was that smudged fingerprint.

"It was a big fingerprint," I told the others, as I munched on Fritos and made notes in my notebook.

"That means it was probably an adult, not one of the other kids," mused Grace. "And it was probably a man, since women have smaller hands." I gave her an admiring look. She really was a good detective.

"A man?" asked Kristy. "Like — like maybe

Mr. Kleinman?" He was still her prime suspect. "I just think he has something important at stake in this contest," she went on.

"A lot of people do," Grace said. "Like, what about that Mrs. Downey? I think she might just keel over and die if her 'Precious' doesn't win!"

We cracked up. But Grace was right. Mr. Kleinman wasn't the only adult who cared about the outcome of the contest.

We talked some more, about how somebody might have gotten to Logan's team's oven in order to change the setting; about who might have switched ingredients on Mari and Grace and caused the fire; even about what Jackie Rodowsky might have been up to both days.

By the time Grace said she had to leave (which was when our BSC meeting was due to start), we hadn't figured out anything for sure. But I felt as if I'd made a new friend.

Later that night, Mary Anne called me to say that she still hadn't heard from her grandmother. "What are we going to *do*, Claud?" she wailed.

I tried to calm her down. "Maybe she'll still call," I said. "We don't need the recipe until tomorrow afternoon. We have some time left."

I could tell that Mary Anne felt better by the time we hung up. But I didn't. I called Shea to fill him in on what was happening, and then I stayed up late that night, working on another of my made-up recipes, just so we'd have something to bake in case Mary Anne's grandmother didn't call us in time. This time it was a plain, easy recipe that would be hard to botch: a yellow cake with chocolate frosting between the layers and white chocolate on the outside. But only the inside would be plain. The look of it would still be artistic. I planned to put a fancy design on top, made with dark chocolate. I worked on that design until I felt my eyelids drooping.

When I finally climbed into bed, the design was finished. But I was still worried. I hoped Mary Anne's grandmother would come through with that recipe, since it sounded like a winner. But even if she did, would we be able to bake it without somebody sabotaging our efforts? And what about Grace? Was she really as nice as she seemed? Or had we made a huge mistake in trusting her? For a while that afternoon I'd been able to forget that she was Cokie's friend. But she was. And Cokie could *never* be trusted.

I had a hard time shutting off my mind that night, but finally I fell asleep. Before I knew it, the sun was shining in my window. It was Saturday morning, and in a few hours my team would have its last chance to make the finals in the Battle of the Bakers.

CHAPTER 9

Saturday

Well, Kidz Kitchen is nearly ready to open, which is a good thing, since tomorrow is our big day. (Kidz Kitchen is the name the kids came up with for our restaurant.) I think the parents will get a big kick out of eating at their kids' restaurant, and I know the kids are getting a big kick out of planning it. Now, if we can just make it through *tomorrow without any major disasters — which may mean keeping a very close eye on a certain Miss Megan...*

I was at the day-care center that morning, but I have to say that I can't recall much of anything that went on. Kristy, Jessi, Dawn, and Mary Anne were there (Stacey, Shannon, and Mal had other sitting jobs), and I let them run the show. I was in charge of caring for the babies, and they both napped for a lot of the morning. While I watched over them, I brooded and worried and fretted about that afternoon's round in the Battle of the Bakers.

Would Mary Anne, Shea, and I have to make my recipe, or would Mary Anne's grandmother come through at the last minute? If her grandmother did come through, would the recipe be any good? (It was hard to imagine how *any* cake could be as good as this one was supposed to be. I wondered if Mr. Spier's memory was playing tricks on him.) What about ingredients? How were we supposed to know what to bring to the afternoon session? And — and what about *sabotage?* Even if we had the best recipe in the world, it could be ruined if we turned our backs for a second.

There were a bunch of other things I was worried about, from whether I'd remembered to bring an extra set of pot holders (we'd needed them badly the weekend before) to what I could say to Mickey, on the Cute Boy team, that might let him know I liked him and wouldn't mind a date. Anyway, I was so preoccupied with my *own* thoughts that I didn't pay a whole lot of attention to what was going on around me that morning. Later, when I read Jessi's notes in the BSC notebook and talked to her and the others, I found out that it had been a pretty wild morning.

First of all, we had a full house that morning. Every single child we thought might show up, did show up. They started to trickle in at about eight, soon after my friends and I had set things up, and they didn't stop coming all morning. Emily was there, with her brother Tyler. Nichole and *her* brother Tyler were there, as well as Tyler's twin Taylor. I spotted Morgan running around, and of course I was watching over her baby sister Dana. Kyle and Megan were on hand, and so were Carolyn and Marilyn, Charlotte, Kerry, and Hannie and Linny. Jamie was there (so was Lucy — she was with me), and so were Jackie, Archie, and Shea. The Rodowskys had even brought some cousins with them: Joseph, who was five, and Julie, who was three. They were visiting from Michigan.

As I said, my babies napped for most of the morning, which was amazing, considering all the noise in that room. I don't know how babies do it. I guess they can sleep through an earthquake. I saw Dana twitch once when Jackie let out a bunch of Tarzan yells, and I noticed that Lucy's eyelids fluttered when Taylor and Tyler had a shoving match and knocked over a stack of folding chairs. But neither of them woke up, even later on when the kids started a marching band, organized by Kristy and Jessi.

They started it toward the end of the morning, mainly because the kids seemed to have a ton of energy that had to be released. By then the restaurant was nearly ready for the next day, and the kids were "bouncing off the walls with excitement," as Jessi said.

Kristy and Jessi had another reason for organizing the marching band. They needed a distraction after what happened to the terrarium. They didn't want the kids to focus on that. But I'm getting ahead of myself. I'll go back and tell it the way Jessi told me.

As usual, Kristy had come up with a plan for the day. She knew there would be a lot of kids on hand, and she also knew there was a lot to do if Kidz Kitchen was going to become a reality. So, as the kids drifted in that morning, Kristy separated them into three groups: chefs, waiter and waitresses, and management.

The chefs — Emily, Morgan, Marilyn, Charlotte, Jamie, Kyle, and Jackie — were checking out ingredients and practicing how to put them together. Kristy and Dawn had spent a lot of time during the week figuring out good recipes that didn't require cooking, refrigeration, or sharp knives. (That hadn't been easy, even with the help of some kids' cookbooks from the library. The Kidz Kitchen menu was going to be heavy on peanut butter.)

The waiter and waitresses — Megan, Linny, Hannie, and Carolyn — were practicing taking orders. Mary Anne had visited an office supply store and found some restaurant order pads, and the kids were thrilled with them. They were running around asking everyone in sight, "What can I bring you, sir?" and "Anything else, ma'am?" and scribbling on their pads.

And the managers were making menus, figuring out prices, and setting up tables so that the restaurant would be ready to open the next day. Kristy helped Kerry and Big Tyler (as we were now calling him) shift chairs, while Jessi worked with Archie, Joseph, Julie, Taylor, and

Little Tyler, who were drawing decorations on the menus she'd written up.

Suddenly, just as Jessi was in the middle of helping Archie find a purple marker, she heard a loud crash. "What was *that*?" she asked, jumping to her feet. She scanned the room, but so many kids were running around that she couldn't figure out what had happened.

"Probably just those chefs," said Kristy with a grin. She nodded toward the counter space where the kids were working. "I bet they're throwing fruit around, or maybe Jackie dropped a tray or something."

"You must be right," said Jessi. "We'll let Dawn and Mary Anne deal with it." She went back to hunting through the box of art supplies (I'd brought a ton of stuff), found the marker, and gave it to Archie so he could start decorating a menu.

She was checking on the other kids in her group when she felt someone tugging on her sleeve. She turned to see Kyle looking up at her. "Hi," she said.

He didn't respond to her smile. Instead, he pulled her aside. "Did you hear that crash before?" he asked in a low voice.

Jessi nodded. "We couldn't figure out what it was," she said.

Kyle hesitated. "It — it was the terrarium," he murmured, looking down at his shoes. "Megan broke it. Then she put the whole mess into the cupboard."

Jessi put her hand over her mouth. "The terrarium!" she said with a groan. "Oh, no."

The terrarium was a beautiful one that belonged in the faculty lounge. It was in a large fish tank, and it was full of healthy, green plants. When we had set up the day-care center, we moved the terrarium from its place of honor on the windowsill behind the couch and put it on top of a waist-high cupboard around the corner from the main part of the lounge, where there was a row of hooks for teachers' coats. We knew the kids would be attracted to it, and we were worried that it would be damaged if they played with it. Having it out of the way wasn't enough for Kristy, though. She'd made a "don't touch" rule and made sure all the kids understood that it was off limits. So far, they'd been pretty good about obeying.

Jessi grabbed Kristy and told her what had happened. Then they asked Logan to keep an eye on their group, and checked out the damage.

"Wow!" said Kristy, when they opened the cupboard door.

"What a mess!" added Jessi. "And what a shame."

One shelf of the cupboard was covered with black, crumbly soil and already wilting plants. The terrarium's frame had come apart, and its plastic sides had collapsed. After a quick look, Kristy shut the door again. "Let's leave this for a minute," she said. "I want to find Megan and ask her what happened."

Jessi and Kristy headed back into the main room, but Megan was nowhere in sight. "Do you know where your sister is?" Jessi asked Kyle, who was making a peanut butter and apple sandwich.

He shook his head. "Some kids went outside," he said. "Maybe she went with them. I just hope she doesn't run away."

Jessi and Kristy rushed outside and found Dawn supervising the waiters and waitresses, who had decided to practice in the courtyard. Jessi sighed with relief when she saw that Megan was in the group. She and Kristy took Megan back inside.

"We just found out about the terrarium," Kristy said as they walked toward the cupboard. "I'm sure it was a mistake, but you're going to have to help us clean up the mess."

"What?" asked Megan. Jessi said later that she looked bewildered. "What terrarium?"

"You know," Jessi said gently. "The one you weren't supposed to touch?" She pointed to the top of the cupboard where the terrarium usually sat.

"I didn't!" said Megan. "I don't know what you're talking about."

"Oh, Megan," said Kristy with a sigh. She opened the cupboard door, and the three of them stared at the mess inside. "Don't make it worse than it already is. Kyle told us what happened."

"Oh. Kyle," said Megan. "He told you?"

Jessi and Kristy nodded.

"Well, I guess that's it, then," said Megan, looking downcast. "I confess. I did it. And I'll help clean up, but can I just go to the bathroom first?"

Jessi told me that Megan seemed surprisingly unemotional about her confession. But she and Kristy were so glad the confrontation was over that they just accepted it. They exchanged glances over Megan's head, and Jessi could tell that she and Kristy were remembering what Kyle had said. If Megan went to the bathroom alone, she might run away.

"Sure, you can go to the bathroom," Kristy said. "I'll come with you."

"And I'll start cleaning up," said Jessi.

Kristy and Megan left, and Jessi started to

pick carefully through the dirt, pulling out plants that might be saved.

"I guess you found her," Kyle said, from behind Jessi.

"We did," said Jessi. "Thanks for your help."

"Megan — " began Kyle haltingly. "Megan does bad things, and she lies a lot. Ever since our dad went away. I don't know why." He looked so upset that Jessi stopped what she was doing to give him a hug. Kyle seemed like such a sweet kid, and he was so concerned about his sister. Jessi promised herself that she would try to help Megan. Maybe, together with Kyle, they could figure out what was making her unhappy enough to lie and steal.

CHAPTER 10

"Are you ready, bakers? Today is the last day of qualifying rounds in the Mrs. Goode's Cookware Battle of the Bakers. At the end of today's judging, only five finalists will be left to compete for the top prizes. Good luck to you all. Now, ready, set, bake!"

Grace and I looked at each other across the dividers. I pointed to my eye and she smiled and nodded and gave me the thumbs-up. We had made a pact to keep an eye out for sabotage that day. I smiled back at her. The pact was still on.

It was hard to believe that a friend of Cokie's could be a friend of mine, but because of the dirty tricks going on at the Battle of the Bakers, I needed all the friends I could find. Mary Anne, Shea, and I really wanted to make it into the finals and have a crack at winning that prize money. Plus, I was having fun with our baking, and I wanted the chance to prove we could make something beautiful *and* delicious. The problem was that everybody else in that room felt the same way — and somebody was willing to do whatever it took to make sure the judges called his or her name at the end of the day.

"Well," I said, turning to face Mary Anne and Shea. I tried to put a lot of enthusiasm into my voice. "I guess it's time to start!" I rubbed my hands together nervously.

"I guess it is," said Mary Anne.

"What do we do first?" asked Shea.

Neither of them sounded very happy. I knew why, too. We hadn't heard from Mary Anne's grandmother, and we were stuck with another one of my recipes. Again. Even though I was pretty sure that this latest one would at least be edible, it was hard to be optimistic about our chances for making the finals. After our not-so-great showings last weekend, we needed a totally awesome dessert for this last day of semifinals. We needed a cake that would look great and also knock the judges' socks off with just one bite. It wasn't likely that my recipe could do all that, but we had no choice. All we could do was try, and hope for the best.

"I set everything up already," I said, gesturing toward the counter. I'd arrived at our workstation early that day — only Julie and

Marty were there before me — and made sure that all our ingredients were laid out neatly in the order in which we'd be using them. "So I guess we can start measuring. Let's see, now." I bent over to check the recipe.

Suddenly I heard Mary Anne gasp. "Dad!" she said. "What are *you* doing here?" I looked up and saw her glancing nervously from her father, who was walking toward our station, holding a grocery bag, to Marty, Kristy, and the judges, who were hanging around on the sidelines. "You're not supposed to — " she began, but he shushed her.

"It's okay," he said. "I've cleared it with the judges. They said it was all right for me to bring you this stuff."

"But what is it?" Mary Anne asked.

"It's the ingredients for Alma's chocolate-cherry cake," he said, grinning. "Your grandmother called me with the recipe after you left this morning." He held up a piece of paper covered with scribbles.

"You're kidding!" said Mary Anne. She grabbed the paper and started to read through it. "This is fantastic. And just in the nick of time." She turned to me. "Your icing design will still work perfectly with this cake," she said.

"Thanks, Mr. Spier," said Shea as he took the bag and started to unload it.

I cleared some of the ingredients for my cake off the counter. I was relieved that we wouldn't have to make my cake after all. "We owe you one," I told Mary Anne's father.

"Just save me a piece of that cake," he said. "I've been craving it for a long, long time now."

"We'll make you a whole cake of your own," promised Mary Anne. She glanced again at the judges. "But you'd better be going, or we'll get in trouble." She gave her father a huge hug. "Thanks again, Dad," she said. "You're the best."

"Good luck!" he called, as he left. "If that cake is anywhere near as good as I remember, you'll be sure to win."

I saw some of the other contestants watching us closely, but I ignored them. We had a cake to make. "Okay, Mary Anne," I said, as soon as her father had left. "What do we do first?"

"An ingredient check," she said. "I'll read down the list and you guys tell me if everything's here." She started to read. "Flour. Butter. Eggs. Sugar."

"Check, check, check, check," said Shea, after he found the ingredients.

"Hold on a second," I said. "Look at that sugar!" I pointed to the bag.

"What?" asked Mary Anne. "It looks like there's plenty."

"Plenty of *what*?" I asked. "This isn't the same bag I put out here. Mine had a yellow price tag on top."

"Maybe my dad brought some new sugar," said Mary Anne.

"Maybe," I said. "But let's check this out, just in case." I opened the bag, stuck in a spoon, and took a taste. "Bleagghh!" I shuddered. "Ew! That's *salt*."

Mary Anne, Shea, and I looked at each other. We hadn't even started baking yet, and already the sabotage had begun. "Somebody must have switched it when we were busy with my dad," said Mary Anne.

I ran to Grace's station and told her what had happened. She and Mari looked shocked. "I didn't see a thing," said Grace. "I mean, there have been lots of parents marching in and out, but nobody came near your station, as far as I saw." She picked up a bag of sugar. "Why don't you use ours?" she asked. "We've already measured out what we need."

I took the sugar. Two weeks ago, I would never have trusted a friend of Cokie's, but I'd learned a lot about Grace, and I knew she wouldn't do anything to mess up our chances of making the finals. "Thanks, Grace," I said. "You saved my team's life." (I could have sworn I heard Cokie groan from her bed.)

I brought the sugar to Mary Anne and headed for the locker room, so I could rinse that salty taste out of my mouth. And just as I turned the corner, guess who I bumped into? Jackie Rodowsky — with flour all over the front of his green T-shirt. "Jackie!" I said, catching him before he could run off. "What are you up to?"

"N-nothing," he said.

"You haven't been fooling around with other people's things, have you?" I asked.

"No!" he said. "I just — I just wanted to build my very own cake. A lady gave me some stuff to use. I can be a cook, too, just like Shea!" He led me to a corner of the locker room, where he'd been working on his "cake." I saw a forlorn, grayish lump sitting on a plate, and my heart melted. He was trying so hard, just like I was.

"Jackie," I said, squatting down so I could look him in the eye. "Someday soon you and I can bake a cake together, okay? But for now, you need to head back to the day-care center. I bet your sitters are wondering where you are." I walked him to the center and watched him go in. Then, shaking my head, I returned to my workstation and started to tell Mary Anne that we could scratch Jackie off our suspect list.

"Claud," she said, interrupting me before I'd finished. "You won't believe what happened while you were gone." She lowered her voice. "Somebody replaced all of Logan's team's eggs with hard-boiled ones!"

"Oh, no." I groaned.

"They had to send someone to buy some more," said Shea. "If they're lucky, they'll still make it in time."

"This is ridiculous!"

"I know," said Mary Anne. "Now I'm suspicious of everybody. I've been watching the parents come and go. Julie's parents have been hovering around all day. Plus, I just saw Mr. Kleinman bring Rachel a bag of sugar, and I could *swear* I saw a bag already on their counter when I walked by a few minutes ago."

"Okay, look," I said. "This is getting out of hand. But there's nothing we can do about it now, except to keep a very close eye on our own ingredients. I think we should just concentrate on putting our recipe together. Once it's in the oven, we'll be safe."

"As long as nobody messes with our oven temperature," said Shea.

"Or our timer," added Mary Anne.

I never knew how stressful baking could be! We mixed our batter as carefully as we could, watching constantly for any suspicious behavior. Finally, we stuck it into the oven. Mary

Anne volunteered to keep an eye on it while Shea and I washed up.

We brought the bowls, spoons, and measuring cups into the locker room and went to work on them. While we were in there, I overheard a lot of people talking about the sabotage, but nobody seemed to have any idea who was responsible. And everybody was nervous about making the finals. "Julie's been biting her nails," said her teammate Celeste, who was at the sink next to ours. "I think her parents are practically going to disown her if she doesn't make the cut."

I felt bad for Julie. Who needed the extra pressure? I knew my parents would be proud of me if I did well in the contest, but they wouldn't be upset if I lost.

Shea and I returned just as our timer rang. Mary Anne pulled out the cake — and it looked perfect.

"Smells delicious," said Shea.

"Now for the frosting," I said. I started to measure and stir. I felt confident. By the time the frosting was ready, the cake was cool enough to ice. I decorated it carefully, and when it was done, it looked awesome, if I do say so myself.

Mary Anne gazed at it. "I have a feeling this cake is a winner," she said happily.

Guess what? She was right.

The judges *loved* our recipe. "This is a real, old-fashioned cake," said one of them.

"So moist! Mrs.Goode would be proud," said another.

"And so beautiful," said a third. All Mary Anne, Shea, and I could do was grin when they told us to come back the next day.

Logan's team made the cut, too, which made Mary Anne happy. So did Julie's (I hoped her parents were happy) and Rachel's. Grace's team was the last finalist named. Sabotage and all, the five best teams had made it through the first rounds. Now we were on our way to the finals!

CHAPTER 11

"Pepperoni!"

"No, sausage!"

"What about extra cheese?"

"I vote for anchovies!"

"EWWWW!"

The people talking were, in order, Grace, me, Mary Anne, Logan, and — *everybody*. Hardly anybody really likes anchovies, except maybe Kristy and her friend Bart. For everyone else, they're just a big joke. Mentioning them always gets a huge reaction.

As you've probably guessed, we were talking about pizza toppings. And we were talking about toppings because we were sitting around a table (actually two tables pushed together) at Pizza Express, about to order a couple of pies. Eight of us were there, so it was taking awhile to decide what to order.

Going to Pizza Express had been my brilliant idea. I thought of it after the finalists were

99

named that Saturday afternoon, and I immediately turned to Mary Anne. "I'm hungry," I said. "I bet everybody else is, too. And I'm dying to figure out who's behind the sabotage. Let's ask everybody we know who's been a victim of sabotage if they want to go out for a pizza." Mary Anne thought this was a great idea, and she talked with Logan and his team. I went Grace's and Mari's workstation, where they were doing a final cleanup, and invited them. And that's how we ended up around those two tables.

Figuring out toppings was like doing one of those impossible math problems about sets and subsets. Logan likes pepperoni, but not onions. Kerry insists on onions, and hates peppers. Mary Anne loves plain old extra cheese with nothing on it, while I like as many toppings as possible (except, of course, those A-things). Shea goes for sausage and onions, and he'd really rather not have pepperoni. Austin and Grace both like peppers and onions, and hate sausage. And Mari voted for — are you ready? — *broccoli*.

We ended up ordering two large pies, one with half pepperoni, half peppers and onions, and the other with half sausage and onions and half extra cheese. The waitress promised to bring Mari some broccoli on the side.

While we sipped our sodas and waited for

the pizzas, we talked about how exciting it had been to make the finals.

"I thought I was going to die when that judge took so long to announce the fifth finalists," said Mari. She toyed with the paper from her straw. "I had my fingers crossed so hard they hurt."

"Me too," said Grace. "But we made it! You should have heard Cokie scream when I called her from the pay phone in the hall. She went totally ballistic."

"Logan was sure we were going to make it," said Kerry timidly, "but I wasn't. I was nervous." She and Shea were the youngest people at the table, and I think they both felt a little shy.

"I was nervous, too," said Austin, giving her a warm smile. "But I knew we'd done our best. I was just worried because we had to work so fast to finish our recipe after I discovered those hard-boiled eggs."

"What *about* those eggs?" I said, narrowing my eyes. "This sabotage is nasty business. I was watching everything today, and stuff still happened. And now we're in the final round."

"That's right," said Grace. "The stakes are higher. And if the person doesn't care about whether he starts fires in people's ovens, who knows what he might do next?"

"Do you think we're in danger?" Mary Anne

asked. I saw her gulp. Logan reached over and squeezed her hand.

"Excuse me!" said the waitress, who appeared just then with two steaming trays in her hands. We all moved our soda cups so she'd have room to put the pizzas down. "Here you go. Enjoy!" She set the trays in the middle of the table.

There was no talking after that. Pizza has a way of cutting a conversation short. It's so delicious, and so hot, and so cheesy and chewy. It demands your full attention.

After a while, I put down a piece of crust. "That was great. I'm stuffed."

"Me too," said Kerry.

"Not me!" said Logan, taking one of the last pieces. But I noticed that he was eating a lot more slowly.

Finally, when all the pizza was gone, and the waitress had taken away the empty trays, we went back to the subject of sabotage.

"Okay," I said, leaning forward and looking at each person at the table in turn, "let's put all our cards on the table." I'd heard somebody say that once, on a TV show, and thought it sounded cool. I'd always wanted the chance to say it myself.

"Huh?" asked Shea. "You want to play cards?"

"No, no," I said. "It's an expression. It

means let's all be honest and tell everything we know. For example, I have to admit that when my team was sabotaged on the first day of the contest, I was pretty sure I knew who had done it." I gave Grace and Mari an apologetic look. "But I was wrong, and I'm sorry."

"I'm sorry, too," said Grace. "I thought *you* sabotaged *us*."

"I had my suspicions, too," admitted Logan. "Like, when both my team and Mary Anne's were sabotaged, I thought maybe Cokie was behind it. But then you guys were sabotaged, too." He nodded at Grace and Mari.

"Cokie wouldn't do that," Grace murmured.

"I wonder if the order of people sabotaged means anything," Austin said. "Like, who was first, and who was second."

We all took sips of soda and thought for a moment. My mind was a blank.

"I know!" said Shea. He sat up straight in his chair. "I was just thinking about how everybody's workstations looked that first day. Ours was really, really neat. So was Logan's team's. But Mari's and Grace's was a mess."

"What are you saying?" asked Mari. "I mean, I can't deny that our station was messy, but that's just how I cook. What does that have to do with anything?"

"Well," said Shea, "just by looking at those three workstations, anybody would have thought that our team and Logan's team really had it together — that we'd probably be better cooks. So they'd target us first."

"Yes!" I said suddenly. "It fits! It's a pattern. Whoever is behind this is out to mess up the best cooks. See?"

"No," said Mari, shaking her head. "I'm not sure I do."

"Well, who won at the end of that first day?" I asked her.

"We did," she said. "With our sticky buns."

"Right," I said. "And whose oven was on fire first thing the next day?"

"Whoa!" said Mari.

"Are you saying we were targeted because we won?" Grace asked.

"That's exactly what I'm saying."

"So the troublemakers must be paying close attention to the judge's scores," Logan said thoughtfully.

"Not only that," added Mary Anne, "they're paying close attention to what kind of supplies we're using. I mean, that sugar bag today? The one somebody filled with salt? It looked *exactly* like the sugar we were using."

"Which means," Austin said slowly, "that the person who does these things plans them carefully beforehand."

Logan was nodding. "Definitely premeditated," he said. "You know, like in one of those courtroom shows. If a person planned a crime, they'd be in more trouble for it than if they did it on the spur of the moment."

Just then, our waitress stopped by to ask if there was anything else she could bring us. I ordered another soda, and so did Mari and Logan. I sipped the last drops of my first soda while I waited for my second. "Doesn't it seem strange, in a way, that we were the only ones sabotaged?" I asked. "I mean, other people there were definitely good bakers. Even people who didn't make the finals."

"Like Mickey and Joey?" Mary Anne asked, teasing.

I could feel myself blushing. "Well, they *were* good bakers," I said. I didn't add that they were cute, too. I'd exchanged phone numbers with Mickey, and I was hoping I'd see him again someday. "Remember those peanut-butter chocolate bars they made? Mmmm!"

"You're right," said Mary Anne. "There were a lot of good bakers in the contest. And you know what? I bet some of them were sabotaged, but they didn't even realize it."

"Wow!" said Logan. "I bet that's true. Like with Mickey and Joey. The day after they made those peanut butter things, they made a chocolate truffle cake. It looked great, but I saw the judges' faces when they tasted it. And, now that I think of it, I heard one of them comment on how bitter it was."

"I bet you anything somebody switched unsweetened chocolate for the semi-sweet kind," I said. "I used the stuff in a brownie recipe once, by mistake, and the brownies were terrible." Thinking about it, I could almost taste these brownies. Ew. I took a sip of my new soda, which the waitress had just brought.

"And what about Sara Hill's team?" asked Kerry. "I tried their muffins last Sunday, and they were great. But I tasted the cake they made today, and it was awful. It had way too much salt in it."

"Maybe somebody messed with their recipe," said Austin. "You know, like if somebody changed a little 't' to a big 'T', they might have put in a tablespoon of salt instead of a teaspoon. They're all pretty young, and they probably aren't experienced bakers, so they wouldn't realize that a tablespoon was a lot of salt for that recipe."

"We're dealing with a devious criminal mind," I said dramatically.

"We sure are," Logan said with a sigh. "I just wish the finals could go smoothly tomorrow, with everything fair and square."

We nodded. "But what can we do about it?" I asked.

"All we can do is keep watching everything that happens," said Grace.

"And I think we should arrive really early tomorrow," Austin added. "When people first come by to drop off their supplies. That way, maybe we can prevent some precontest sneaking around."

"Good idea," I said. Everybody agreed. Shea, who's good at that sort of thing, divided up our check. Then we took our last sips of soda and left Pizza Express. I think we all felt a little more hopeful. Maybe, just maybe, we'd have a chance at catching the person responsible for the sabotage, now that we were working as a team. We wished each other luck as we said goodbye, and I realized that now I almost hated the thought of competing against them. *Almost*.

CHAPTER 12

Wham!

Slam!

"What was that?" Logan asked.

"Don't know," I said, rubbing my eyes. I was still sleepy. We had arrived at the high school super early. "We better go see, though," I added. After all, we'd come to do detective work.

Mary Anne was there, too, and so were Shea, Austin, and Kerry. Grace and Mari hadn't arrived yet, but I expected them any minute. We were standing around near the side entrance to the gym, the one most people had been using during the Battle of the Bakers.

"It sounded like it came from the back parking lot. I think it was car doors slamming," said Shea. "Let's go look." He headed off at a trot, and we followed him.

Just as I was rounding the corner of the building, Shea stopped short and backed up, holding up his hand. "Wait!" he hissed. "Don't let them see you."

I heard Mary Anne, who was in front of me, gasp when she saw what Shea was looking at. She exchanged surprised glances with Logan.

I peeked over her shouder. "Oh, my lord," I whispered. "This is interesting."

"What?" asked Kerry, jumping up and down as she tried to see over *my* shoulder.

I let her slip in front of me. Austin was standing beside me, so I knew he could see. We watched as the little scene in front of us played itself out. The characters? Julie Liu and Marty Nisson. The setting? A small red car. (They had apparently just climbed out of it, and they were now standing in front of it.) The action? Julie was tucking a set of keys into her pocketbook while Marty waited for her.

I know what you're thinking. So far, this isn't the most exciting scene. But wait. What happened next made Mary Anne give another, much louder, gasp.

Marty and Julie kissed. And when I say that, I mean they really *kissed*. There was, like, major lip contact. And it lasted for what seemed like minutes. It was a kiss from the movies.

"Wow," breathed Mary Anne, after we'd watched Julie and Marty finish their kiss and head for the back door of the gym. "I guess they're in love."

I could tell she was caught up in the romance of it, but I had other things on my mind. "This puts a whole new light on things," I said, frowning. "Don't forget that our pal Marty is one of the people running the contest. And now we find out that he's involved with one of the contestants. Isn't that a little suspicious?"

"You mean you think Marty is the one who's been sabotaging everyone?" said Austin. "But he's such a nice guy."

I shrugged. "I agree," I said. "I'd hate to think he was the one. But didn't you see the way he looked at her?"

"Sure," said Logan. "I saw it. So what?"

"He looked like a prince in a fairy tale." Mary Anne sighed.

"Exactly," I said. "He looked like a prince in love. A prince so in love that he might do *anything* to make sure his princess gets her heart's desire — which is to win this contest!"

"Marty wouldn't do that!" Logan said. Then he frowned and thought for a second. "I mean, he just wouldn't." A pause. "Would he?"

"I hope not," said Kerry. "I like Marty."

"We all like Marty," I said. "But we're going to have to treat him as a suspect from now on. That means keeping an eye on him at all times." I was wishing I could think of something else to do besides keeping an eye on him, or on any other suspect we might find. We needed a plan. A way to catch the person who'd been trying to mess up our chances of winning the contest. I had been up half the night before, thinking and thinking (and wishing I hadn't eaten quite so much pizza), but I hadn't come up with a single idea. At one point, I had even turned on my light and dug out some Nancy Drews to comb through for ideas. But Nancy hadn't been able to help.

"Hey, what's that?" Shea said, interrupting my train of thought. "I think I just heard another car drive up, back by the side entrance. Let's check out who else is here." Once again, he set off at a trot and the rest of us followed behind.

This time, there were no big surprises. The latest arrivals were Rachel and Anna, plus Mr. Kleinman, who had driven them. He pulled up to the curb, parked, and followed them as they walked toward the door, talking all the way. From what I could hear, he was giving the girls last-minute tips and directions. He seemed nervous, but his tension was nothing compared to his daughter's. She looked totally stressed-out.

"I don't know, Dad," she kept saying. But he seemed to be reassuring her, over and over again.

As they passed the spot where we were standing (we were doing our best to act naturally), I smiled at Rachel and said hi. She gave me a timid little smile in return, but didn't say anything. She was too busy listening to her father, who was still lecturing as they headed for the entrance.

The last thing I heard her say to him was this: "I'm sure I won't win."

And the last thing I heard *him* say was this: "I'm sure you will, honey. I'm absolutely sure."

Hmm. I turned to Mary Anne to see if she'd heard what I'd heard. Her eyes were big and round, so I figured she had.

"He sounds like he knows what he's talking about," said Logan. So he'd heard it, too.

"He sure does," I replied. "He sounds like he knows something the rest of us don't know."

"Like, how his daughter is going to be the only possible winner today?" asked Austin.

"Could be," I said. "I guess we have two major suspects now."

Just then, Grace's dad dropped Grace and Mari off. Everybody started talking to them at once, filling them in on what we'd seen. Me? I let the others explain. I wanted one more chance to come up with a plan. I started to think again about the Nancy Drew books I've read. All these detective terms popped into my head, such as "stakeout" (we'd already done that, by arriving early), and "eavesdrop" (we'd done that, too, when Rachel and her dad walked by). Finally, I thought of one that fit: "scene of the crime." Detectives talk about how criminals return to the scene of the crime. And, in this case, if the criminal wanted to do his job, he'd *have* to return to the scene of the crime.

In other words, if somebody wanted to knock me and my team out of the contest, they were going to have to do it by sabotaging our recipe. And to do that, they would have to visit our workstation. All we had to do was catch them in the act. "Hey!" I said out loud. Actually, I guess I shouted it, because everybody turned to look at me, and they all wore very surprised expressions.

"What is it, Claud?" asked Mary Anne.

"I have it! A plan!" I could hardly wait to tell them. "Everybody come close," I said, waving them toward me. When we had formed a huddle, I started talking. "Here's what we'll do. . . ."

As soon as I arrived in the faculty lounge, I told the other BSC members our plan. We would need everybody's help. After that, the morning sped by. The kids were wildly busy, preparing for their restaurant, but I didn't get involved. Once again, I volunteered to watch the babies, and once again, the babies napped. That gave me plenty of time to fine-tune my plan. By the time the adult division finished up and we headed into the gym for our final day of the Battle of the Bakers, I was ready.

The place looked a little different, since only five teams were still involved. Some of the workstations had been taken apart, for example. And it was quieter. There was a serious feeling in the air.

I headed for a workstation on one end of the row, and just as I claimed it I saw Grace claiming the one across from it. I gave her the thumbs-up sign. So far, our plan was right on target.

Dawn, who had followed me in, pretending to help me carry groceries, raised her eyebrows at me. I tilted my head toward the back of the gym. She followed my glance, then looked at me and nodded. Casually, she wove her way over to where Mr. Kleinman was standing. I knew she would carry out her part of the plan perfectly.

What she was supposed to do was start talking with Mr. Kleinman, and "accidentally" let it drop that my team had a "foolproof" recipe for the finals. (The idea was that this would push him into sabotaging us, if he really were the criminal.)

Meanwhile, Kristy, who was still on Cake Cop duty, was doing the same thing with Marty. We were all set.

Mary Anne, Shea, and I went ahead and mixed our batter as quickly as possible. (We were making the chocolate-cherry cake again, since it had been so successful.) When the batter was ready, Mary Anne poured it into the cake pans.

Now it was Jessi's turn to do her part. She ran into the gym, found Mr. Kleinman, and told him that there was a phone call for him in the principal's office. At the same time, Dawn ran in, grabbed Marty, and told him there was a "crisis" in the day-care center.

Once our two prime suspects were temporarily out of the way, we swung into action. Mary Anne grabbed our cake pans and ran them to Grace's and Mari's station, where she shoved them into the oven. (Shea had arranged this, after checking to see if they were using the same oven temperature for their recipe.)

When she returned to our station, she and Shea and I set to work quickly. We carefully shook out two five-pound bags of flour, covering every surface with a nearly invisible layer of fine white powder. (Since the counters and appliances were white, it hardly showed up.)

"Excuse me," somebody said from behind me, just as we'd finished doing the job. I whirled around and saw one of the judges. She had a peculiar look on her face. "Would you mind telling me what's going on?"

"I'd love to," I said. "But first, I wonder if you could come with me to the station across from us. I think you'll understand soon enough, if you'll just step over there."

CHAPTER 13

Sunday

Things are seldom what they seem.... Once again, that old saying comes true. What happened today should just remind us all not to make assumptions, because the truth is not always right out there on the surface. (How deep and philosophical!) Oh, and by the way, we had a blast with Kidz Kitchen.

Meanwhile, back in the faculty lounge, Kidz Kitchen was in full swing, and Dawn was in the thick of it. All the work the kids had done was paying off. The day-care center had turned into a real, true, operating restaurant! (Well, with a few differences. For example, the patrons were paying for their meals with play money. The parents had already pitched in to pay for ingredients, so we didn't think it was fair to make them pay again for their meals.)

The "restaurant" was packed. Just about all of the adults who had been in the contest stopped in, and Dawn said she thought this helped to distract some of the contestants who hadn't done too well. (Their finals had ended with a surprising win by a grandmother from Brooklyn.) Many of the contestants were hanging around to watch the under-sixteen finals, so they were happy to have a place to grab a bite to eat, whether or not they had kids involved in the project.

The kids were divided up into the same teams Kristy had come up with the day before. The managers — Kerry, Archie, Big Tyler, Joseph, Julie, Taylor, and Little Tyler — were greeting customers, seating them, and making sure they had menus. Even the youngest kids were doing their jobs with real sophistication and seriousness. Dawn made sure to save one of the menus. Here's what it looked like:

MENU

Peanut Butter sandwiches with (choose one or more):
    fresh frute (apples, bananas, or peaches) ... honey ...
    Fluff ... raisins ... coconut flakes ... grape jelly

on
ra isen toast, hole wheat, or white

$ 1. 00

sandwiches can be cut into the shape of a star, heart, or
    gingerbread man
    (10 cents extra)

Bug Salad (not real bugs)............75 cents

Jello Jigglers Orange, lemon, lime, or chery. Assorted zhapes ...... 25 cents

Popcorn (with parmisan cheese or cimmanon + sugar) .... 50 cents

Beverages: Kool-Aid (grape), leminade, or apple juice .... 25 cents

There was something for everyone. In case you're wondering, the "bug salad" was made from half a canned pear, with carrot curls for legs and raisins for eyes. It was adorable, and lots of people ordered it (out of curiosity, probably).

The peanut butter sandwiches were the other big hit. The chefs — Emily, Morgan, Marilyn, Charlotte, Kyle, Jamie and Jackie — went through about five family-sized jars of super chunky. There were no temperamental chefs in Kidz Kitchen, fortunately. Everyone had a great time. And Jackie didn't have a single major accident. (He did have a few minor ones, but nothing a good washing machine couldn't handle.)

And the waiter and waitresses — Megan, Linny, Hannie, and Carolyn — did a terrific job. They were very professional about taking down orders carefully and bringing them to the chefs as quickly as possible. The trickiest part, Dawn told me, was when they had to deliver drinks. There were a few spills, but the customers didn't seem to mind.

Dawn, Stacey, Jessi, and Mal supervised the event, since Mary Anne, Logan, and I were still baking and Kristy was on Cake Cop duty. Dawn and Jessi helped out in the "dining area," where the customers were seated, while

Mal and Stacey worked with the chefs, in the "kitchen," which was really just a few tables plus some counter space, with a sink nearby. The scene was total chaos. "Fortunately, Mrs. Newton and Ms. Singer were both on hand to take care of their own babies," Dawn said. "Otherwise, I don't know how we could have done it."

Dawn and the others had vowed to keep a watchful eye on Megan. And at first, that was easy. Since Megan was a waitress, she spent most of her time shuttling back and forth between the dining area and the kitchen. But after a while, Dawn found that she kept losing track of her. There were just too many kids running around, and too much was going on. Megan's and Kyle's mom had already stopped in for a peanut butter sandwich and a cup of Kool-Aid, but now she was back in the gym, watching the under-sixteen finals. Dawn had thought of talking to her about Megan, but had decided that the noisy restaurant didn't seem like the best place for a confidential chat.

Dawn told me she was busy helping Hannie deliver a tray filled with cups of lemonade when she first heard water spilling. "The sound was unmistakable," she said, "I could hear it clearly, even over the noise in that room." She glanced around to see where it had come from, and saw nothing suspicious. She finished the delivery, then decided to find out what the problem was.

"Oh, no!" she said, when she spotted the overflowing sink. She ran to it and turned off the tap, which had been left on. "Didn't you guys hear that?" she asked as she started to swab up the spilled water with a nearby dishtowel. The young chefs looked up and shook their heads. They were so absorbed in their jobs that they wouldn't have heard a helicopter fly through. "Where's Stacey?" Dawn asked next.

"She's helping Jackie bring out some bug salads," Charlotte answered. "He had a big platter of them all made up."

"Where's Jessi?" Dawn asked. Everybody shrugged. Dawn gave an exasperated sigh and went back to mopping up. Then she felt someone tap her on the shoulder, and she turned to see Kyle standing behind her.

"What is it, Kyle?" she asked, a little impatiently. She had pulled out the rubber stopper that had been stuck in the drain, but water was still slopping all over the place.

"Megan did it," he said.

"Megan did what?" Dawn asked.

"Stopped up the sink and left the water running." Kyle was looking down at the ground and rubbing the toe of one foot into the floor.

Dawn frowned, shook back her hair, pushed up her sleeves, and went on mopping up. "Megan and I are going to have a little talk, as soon as I finish up here," she said firmly.

Just then, Jessi appeared with — guess who? — Megan in tow. "What's up?" she asked Dawn.

"We're having a little problem here," Dawn answered. She gave Megan a Look, the kind of look your mother gives you when she knows you've done something wrong.

"Did the plumbing back up while Megan and I were out?" asked Jessi.

"No, the plumbing didn't back up," Dawn began. "Somebody left the faucet on and plugged — " she stopped short. "Wait, did you say that you and Megan have been out?" she asked Jessi.

Jessi nodded. "For about half an hour. The kitchen ran out of peanut butter, and Megan said she needed a break from waitressing, so we went out to round up some more."

Dawn glanced at Kyle. He looked back at her defiantly. "She left it on a long time ago," he said.

Dawn turned to Megan. "Kyle told me that you were the person who left the water running. Is that true?" Suddenly, Dawn wasn't so sure Megan was the culprit. Could the water really have been running for half an hour before she heard it?

Megan shot a look at Kyle. Then she faced Dawn again. "I did it," she said quietly.

"Megan!" said Jessi. "How could you have — ?"

"I *said* I did it," Megan interrupted her. She glared at Kyle again, then stomped off. Kyle headed off in another direction.

Jessi and Dawn exchanged looks. "Something weird is going on here," said Jessi. "I can't figure Megan out."

"I know," said Dawn. "Maybe I'll go talk to her and see if I can find out what's wrong." She gave one last swipe to the counter, and headed off after Megan. She found her sitting quietly by herself, away from the chaos of the restaurant. "Megan," Dawn began, putting her hand gently on Megan's shoulder, "can you tell me what's bothering you?" Megan shook her head without saying anything. But Dawn felt her take a long, shaky breath. "You didn't leave that sink stopped up, did you?" asked Dawn.

That did it. Megan burst into tears, and Dawn pulled her into a hug. "Okay," she kept saying. "It's okay."

Finally, Megan was able to speak. "I didn't do it," she said. "Kyle did. And he did all those other things, too. Then he covered up by saying *I* did them, and acting all cute and bubbly. He's been doing it ever since our dad left." She sniffed.

"But why did you let him say it was you?" Dawn asked.

"I was afraid that if I didn't, he'd get in trouble, and then maybe he'd try to run away again. He did that once already."

Dawn sighed. She felt somebody standing next to her. She turned to see Kyle, who looked nearly as teary as Megan. "I heard what she told you," said Kyle. "And it's true. I *did* do those things. I'm really, really bad."

"Oh, no, you're not," said Dawn, opening her arms so she could hug him *and* Megan. "You're a good person who's having a bad time. I know how that is, since my parents are divorced. My brother had a real hard time with it, and now he lives with my dad in California. I miss them both so much! Anyway, maybe if I help you two talk to your mom about it, you'll feel a little better. Okay?"

"Okay," said Kyle. His voice was muffled, since his face was hidden in Dawn's shoulder.

"Okay," said Megan, with a sniffle.

And for the rest of the day, they seemed to be able to put their troubles behind them and have a great time helping out with Kidz Kitchen. At one point, Kyle spilled a glass of

Kool-Aid, and Dawn noticed how quickly he apologized and helped to clean it up. He didn't even *try* to blame Megan. Maybe things would be better for them now that everything was out in the open.

CHAPTER 14

"What's going on here, Miss — "the judge consulted her clipboard — "Kishi?"

"You'll understand in a couple of minutes, I promise!" I gave her a pleading look. The judge was standing next to me in Grace's and Mari's station, and she was looking more than a little annoyed. She was a short, plump, blonde woman, the owner of a fancy bakery in Stamford. Her name, according to the name tag she wore, was Anna Salerno.

"But — "

"Shhh!" I said, putting my finger to my lips. "This is about the sabotage!" I couldn't *believe* the way I was talking to the judge, but I was not going to let her blow my plan. And if she didn't quiet down, that's exactly what she was going to do. She gave me a startled look when I shushed her, but at least she did stop trying to ask questions.

I checked my watch. Any second now,

Marty and Mr. Kleinman should be returning to the gym. We figured it would take them five minutes to go to where we'd sent them, two minutes to figure out that they weren't really needed there, and five more minutes to come back. So far, they'd been gone for eleven minutes. My nerves were jangling, now that the moment of truth had almost arrived.

I heaved a big sigh, blowing air up into my bangs, and I crossed two sets of fingers on each hand. (I would have crossed my toes, too, but there was no room in the pointy-toed cowboy boots I was wearing that day.) Under my breath, I started to count: "Ten, nine, eight, seven, six — oh, my lord!"

Marty and Mr. Kleinman had just walked into the gym, a few seconds ahead of schedule. They both looked confused, and Mr. Kleinman looked a little angry, as if he knew we'd pulled a trick on him. I froze when I saw them. What was supposed to happen next? Suddenly I wasn't sure. It was my own plan, and I couldn't even remember the next step! I started to panic, though I managed to hide that from Ms. Salerno. I think Grace and Mari could tell something was wrong, but there was nothing they could do except stand there with me and watch.

Fortunately, Mary Anne and Shea remembered the next part of the plan. They were still standing in our workstation, and they swung into action almost immediately after they'd spotted Mr. Kleinman's and Marty's return to the gym.

"I think we need some water, Mary Anne," Shea said loudly. "How about if I go get some in the locker room?"

All right, Shea! I thought he sounded perfect. You'd never have known that he was reciting a line I'd written for him.

"Fine, Shea," answered Mary Anne, also in a loud voice. "And maybe I'll step outside while you're gone. Now that I've put our cake into the oven, I sure could use some fresh air."

"Yes!" I whispered. Mary Anne had delivered *her* lines perfectly, too. I knew that everybody in the gym must have heard both her and Shea's speeches. To anyone who was listening, it would seem obvious that our whole team would soon be missing from our workstation.

After a second or two, Shea and Mary Anne left the gym. I watched them walk away, and then spun around to face Ms. Salerno. "Turn around," I hissed to her.

She raised her eyebrows, but did as I'd ordered. I turned, too. Now we were both facing away from my team's workstation.

"I don't understand — " she began, but before she could finish I put my hand on her arm to get her attention. Then I pointed to a spot just above our heads. There, where I'd propped it up early that morning, was the hand mirror I usually keep on my dressing table at home. It was perched on the partition wall, and it was aimed directly at my workstation.

"Ohhh!" said Ms. Salerno softly. Then she nodded, and I knew she understood.

With the help of that mirror, we would be able to see whatever happened at my workstation — *without anyone knowing we were watching.*

Within a few seconds, I would know if my plan had worked. Would the rat take the bait? And which rat would it be? I held my breath and waited. I had the feeling that Ms. Salerno was holding her breath, too.

But nothing happened. Our workstation was empty, and it stayed that way.

After a couple of minutes Ms. Salerno turned to me. "I'm going to have to move on," she said.

"Oh, no!" I whispered. "Please wait. *Please?*" I must have sounded like a three-year-old begging for a cookie, but I didn't care. I still thought something might happen, if we watched for a little while longer.

Ms. Salerno shook her head. "My judging duties — " she began.

"Oh! Oh! Oh!"

That was Mari. She was whispering those "oh's," and kind of hopping up and down while she pointed up at the mirror. I followed her gaze.

"Whoa!" Grace said, under her breath.

"Oh, my goodness," Ms. Salerno said, under hers.

"Oh, my lord," I whispered. We were all looking at the same thing. It was the top of a person's head, reflected in the mirror. The person was bending over the counter in our workstation, which is why we were seeing only that black, wavy hair. *Marty*. It was him, I was sure of it. And right away I was sorry. I liked Marty. I didn't want him to be the one responsible for the sabotage.

"He just walked in there, all casual," Mari whispered. "Maybe he's checking something out." I could tell she liked him, too.

As the four of us watched in the mirror, Marty prowled around what we could see of the workstation as if he were looking for something. Then he glanced over his shoulder, leaned across the counter, and adjusted the controls on the oven.

I gasped.

Marty may have heard me gasp. I'll never know. But something made him straighten up quickly. And when he did, he looked down

131

at himself and realized that his hands, his shirt, his pants, and even his shoes were covered with a fine white dusting of flour. Marty had been caught "white-handed." You should have seen the look on his face.

I started to tell Ms. Salerno to follow me, but she was already on her way to our workstation. Marty just stood there, as if he knew he were trapped.

Within what seemed like seconds, a crowd gathered around our workstation. Mary Anne and Shea had reappeared, and I saw Kristy walking toward us. Most of the other judges wanted to see what was going on, and so did many of the contestants.

While an angry Ms. Salerno grilled Marty (I overheard her saying something about his betraying "Mrs. Goode's good name"), I craned my neck to see what Julie was doing. She was still in her workstation, but she looked as if she were about to bolt. I went over to her and asked her, very politely, to join us. She came without resisting.

"I think Julie may know something about what's going on," I said as I pushed her toward Ms. Salerno.

"She's innocent," Marty cried. "It was all my idea! Sure, I wanted her to win. She's my girlfriend, and she's the best baker around. Plus, if she won, maybe her parents would get off her back and let her spend more time with me."

"Fine," I said. "Maybe it *was* all your idea, in the beginning. But Julie isn't exactly innocent. For one thing, she shouldn't even be in this division of the contest."

"What are you saying?" asked a judge.

"I'm saying," I said dramatically, "that she isn't under sixteen!"

Everybody gasped. (That was cool.)

"How do you know?" Mary Anne asked me. She looked as surprised as anyone else. That was because I hadn't told any of my BSC friends what I'd figured out. The main reason I hadn't told them was because it was only a hunch. I wasn't positive. But I had decided to go ahead and act on my hunch.

I folded my arms and turned toward Julie. "Because she was *driving* this morning," I said. "I saw her put the car keys into her bag before she and Marty kissed good-bye." My heart was beating fast. Was my hunch right?

Julie's face crumpled. "It's true," she said. "It's all true."

For a half second I felt as if I were sitting on top of the world. That didn't last, though. How could I feel good when Marty and Julie were in trouble? Neither of them was really a bad person. Marty had done what he had done for love, and Julie went along with it because

133

she felt pressure from her parents. I could relate to that. I gave Julie a sympathetic look. Marty put his arm around her.

"Don't cry," he told her quietly. "It'll be okay." Then he turned to the rest of us. "All I can say is that I'm really, really sorry. What I did was wrong, and even dangerous. I didn't mean to start a fire." He glanced at Grace and Mari.

Mr. Kleinman stepped forward. "I have a suggestion," he said, turning to face the crowd. "What if we try to make the best of things, and go on with the contest?" He gave the air a sniff. "I smell a lot of delicious things baking, and I bet the judges are looking forward to tasting them." He smiled, and I saw several of the judges smile back at him.

Then Ms. Salerno spoke up. "I think Mr. Kleinman has the right idea," she said. "Do the other judges concur?" She looked around, and they nodded. "Good. Then I suggest that the teams go back to their workstations — Claudia, your team will have a little cleaning to do — and finish their entries!"

And that's exactly what we did. Our cake came out of Grace's and Mari's oven just a few minutes later, and by the time Mary Anne brought it back to our workstation, Shea and I had cleaned up most of the flour. When the layers had cooled we filled and iced the cake, and by the time it was done I felt terrific. Not only had we caught the culprit who had been out to ruin the contest, but we had made one great-looking (and, hopefully, great-tasting) cake, too.

The rest of the afternoon flew by. When all the entries were finished (everyone had been given a little extra time), the judges walked around the gym looking at and tasting them, one by one. Then they went off to a corner to confer, while we contestants waited anxiously.

Finally, Ms. Salerno walked to the platform that had been set up in the middle of the gym. She tapped on the microphone to find out if it was on. Then she leaned forward and spoke into it. "Ladies and gentlemen, boys and girls," she said. We had been chattering nervously, but suddenly the gym was silent. "I have here in my hand," she held up a piece of paper, "the results of the Mrs. Goode's Cookware Battle of the Bakers, junior division."

CHAPTER 15

Mary Anne reached over and grabbed my hand. "I'm so nervous," she said.

I smiled at her and gave her hand a squeeze. "Me, too," I replied. "But we did the best we could. And at least we know that whoever wins today won fair and square, right?"

"Right!" said Shea. He was holding Mary Anne's other hand.

"Good luck!" Grace called. She and Mari were standing nearby.

"Good luck to you, too!" I called back. And I meant it.

Ms. Salerno was going on about how the judges had come to their decision. It was as if she wanted to draw out the tension as long as she could. "Come *on!*" I said, under my breath. Mary Anne caught my eye and grinned.

". . . and finally," Ms. Salerno said, "I want to say two things. First of all, this was one of

136

the closest contests I have ever judged. You are excellent bakers! And secondly, I'd like to thank you for dealing in such a mature fashion with the problems we encountered along the way." She glanced in my direction. "This will be one Battle of the Bakers I'll never forget!"

I smiled at her, but under my breath I was still saying "Come *on*! Come *on*!" For the moment, I wanted to forget about the mystery. All I wanted to hear was who had won the contest.

"And now," said Ms. Salerno, taking a deep breath, "the moment you've been waiting for."

"All *right*!" I whispered. "Finally."

She unfolded the piece of paper so slowly I could hardly stand it. I felt this crazy urge to run to her and grab it out of her hands. But then, finally, she began to read from it. "It is my great pleasure to announce — " she paused dramatically, and I held my breath. In a second, I'd know who had won the contest. " — the second runner-up in the Mrs. Goode's Cookware Battle of the Bakers!" Ms. Salerno finished.

I let out my breath. Would my team be named one of the runners-up? And how would I feel if we were? On the one hand, winning second or third place would be terrific. On the other hand, to be honest with myself, I would have to admit that first place would be even better.

I didn't have to wonder for long, though. Ms. Salerno went right ahead and announced the name of the team that had won second runner-up: "Congratulations to Team Eight," she said. "Logan and Kerry Bruno, and Austin Bentley."

A big cheer rose up, and I turned to see that my BSC friends had come into the gym and were standing at the back, along with several kids they were still responsible for. I also saw my parents and Janine, who had come to watch the final judging. I smiled and waved to them.

Mary Anne ran to Logan and gave him a hug, right in front of everybody (which is *not* Mary Anne's style). Logan looked surprised, and even blushed a little. But then he pulled himself together and led Kerry and Austin to the platform to receive the yellow ribbon Ms. Salerno was waiting to give them.

She asked Logan's team to stay where they were until all the winners had been announced. "And now, our first runner-up," she said.

I held my breath again, and recrossed my fingers. First runner-up would be pretty good. If she called my team's name, I knew I'd be happy.

But she didn't. Instead, she announced that Rachel Kleinman and Anna Atamian, Team Five, were the official first runners-up. Rachel and Anna squealed and hugged each other, and I saw Mr. Kleinman beaming as the crowd applauded and Rachel and Anna received their ribbon.

"And now," said Ms. Salerno, after she'd congratulated the girls, "the moment you've *really* all been waiting for."

"And waiting, and waiting," I whispered. Shea giggled. By that time, Mary Anne was holding both our hands again. I noticed that her hand was damp. I guess mine probably was, too. This was it! In a second, we'd either be the winners of the whole contest — or we'd walk away with nothing but memories. "Either way," I whispered to Mary Anne and Shea, "I had a great time with you guys."

Mary Anne immediately became all teary-eyed. I should have known. "Oh, me, too, Claud," she said, in a choked-up voice.

"It was fun," said Shea. He tried to sound cool. But you know what? He was a little choked up, too.

Ms. Salerno cleared her throat. "Again, I just want to say that we judges found it very difficult to choose a winner in this contest. Every entry was delicious. But we agreed that one did rise above the others, in both taste and appearance. That was the chocolate-cherry cake made by Claudia Kishi, Mary Anne Spier, and Shea Rodowsky. Congratulations to our winners, Team Seven!"

I didn't react right away. I couldn't. All I could do was stand there and stare at Ms. Salerno. Thinking back, I'm sure that my mouth was hanging open and that I looked like a total geek. But at the time, I couldn't have cared less what I looked like. I was just trying to take in what Ms. Salerno had said, and for some reason her words did not make sense.

Mary Anne threw her arms around me, and so did Shea. I hugged them back. "We did it!" said Shea.

"We won!" said Mary Anne.

"We did?" I said wonderingly. Then the light came on in my head. "We *did*!" I cried. "We *won*!" I threw my fists in the air. "*Yesss!*" I heard my friends and family cheering.

"Come on up," said Ms. Salerno. "Let me introduce you to Mr. Herriot, President and CEO of Mrs. Goode's Cookware. I believe he has a check for you." A bearded man was climbing the platform.

Shea, Mary Anne, and I shook hands with everybody on the platform, which took a while, since the first and second runners-up were still there, too. After that, the rest of the ceremony passed in a blur. Mr. Herriot handed me a check, and flashbulbs went off. Ms. Salerno hugged Shea, and more flashbulbs went off. Mr. Herriot said something about our recipe being in the cookbook, and then the rest of the judges shook our hands and my friends and family started to swarm all over the platform. Everybody was hugging and saying, "I don't believe it!"

The next thing I knew, I was in the car with my parents and Janine, heading home. They kept saying how proud they were, but I was barely listening. I was too busy fantasizing about how to spend my share of the prize money. I knew my parents would have something to say about it — they'd probably insist that I do something boring, such as put it in my college fund — but I could dream for a little while about clothes and accessories and CD players, couldn't I?

I also dreamed about seeing my name in a real, published book. One that anybody could buy in a bookstore. One that a lot of people probably *would* buy. The idea was cool beyond words. What would the recipe be called? How about Claudia's Classy Chocolate-Cherry Cake? Or maybe something simpler, such as Cake à la Claudia . . .

* * *

"Alma's Memory Cake," Mary Anne said. "I couldn't sleep, so I thought about it all night, and that's the name that finally popped into my head. It's perfect, isn't it? I really wanted to have my mother's name in there."

It was Monday afternoon, and the BSC members were gathered in my room for a meeting. We'd skipped over business, and we were talking about the Battle of the Bakers. Mary Anne had just told us about the name she had come up with for our recipe.

"It's perfect," was all I could say. I felt terrible for even thinking of using my own name. The recipe came from Mary Anne's mother. We owed everything to her — and to Mary Anne's grandmother. Mary Anne had already called her grandmother and thanked her for sending the recipe in time, but then and there I made a promise to myself that I would write a thank-you note of my own to her. Maybe I could make a card with a watercolor of the cake on it.

"My dad thought so, too," said Mary Anne. "He looked like he was going to cry when I told him the name." She looked sad for a second, then grinned. "But he cheered up as soon as I told him I'd be making him a cake of his own tonight. It sure will be fun to bake one in my own house, without having to worry about sabotage!"

"Speaking of sabotage, what happened to Marty?" asked Dawn. "Are they going to throw him in jail, or what?"

"I don't think so," Kristy said. "From what I heard, Mrs. Goode's isn't going to press charges. But I have a feeling Marty's going to be looking for a new job."

"I hope he finds one," I said. "He's a nice guy, just a little confused."

"Sort of like Kyle," said Jessi. (She and Dawn had already told us what had happened.) "He's going to be just fine."

"Once he recovers from eating four peanut butter sandwiches, that is!" Stacey added, laughing. "He and the other kids ended up eating all the leftovers from Kidz Kitchen. I think we sent more than one of them home with a tummy ache yesterday!"

"That reminds me," I said. "Grace called today. Cokie's over her bronchitis. Guess how Grace could tell." I paused, grinning. "She said Cokie's hopping mad about how friendly we became with Grace. She can't believe we ended up on the same side. And she told Grace to tell us that she, Cokie, isn't falling for our tricks. 'The feud isn't over,' is what she said. Grace was laughing when she told me, but I know Cokie wasn't kidding."

"What would the BSC be without Cokie for an enemy?" mused Mary Anne.

"Happy?" asked Jessi.

"Secure?" asked Mal.

"Bored!" exclaimed Kristy. That's when we cracked up. Kristy was right. A lot of things might change in this world, but Cokie Mason probably never will, and I guess that's okay. She adds a certain something to our lives — the same way cherries add something to a chocolate cake.

About the Author

ANN M. MARTIN did *a lot* of baby-sitting when she was growing up in Princeton, New Jersey. She is a former editor of books for children, and was graduated from Smith College.

Ms. Martin lives in New York City with her cats, Mouse and Rosie. She likes ice cream and *I Love Lucy*; and she hates to cook.

Ann Martin's Apple Paperbacks include *Yours Turly, Shirley*; *Ten Kids, No Pets*; *With You and Without You*; *Bummer Summer*; and all the other books in the Baby-sitters Club series.

Look for Mystery #22

STACEY AND THE
HAUNTED MASQUERADE

When I arrived at school first thing that
Wednesday morning, Todd Long met me near
the side door. "You won't believe it," he said.
"*I* don't believe it."

"What?" I asked. But Todd wouldn't answer. He just led me through the halls until
we were near the cafeteria. The floor there was
covered with tiny bits of red confetti. "So?" I
asked Todd. "Somebody made some weird
mess here. Is this what you wanted to show
me?"

Todd didn't answer. He just swung his gaze
around at the walls, and I followed it. That's
when it hit me. The posters! That wasn't confetti on the floor. It was Claudia's beautiful
posters for the masquerade — all ripped into
minuscule bits.

I put my hand over my mouth. I couldn't
speak.

"I know," Todd said grimly. "They also tore up the one near the auditorium and the one by the main entrance."

"But — why?" I asked. "What a horrible thing to do!"

"That's not the worst of it," Todd said. "I want you to see something else." He led me through the halls again, this time toward the gym. I had no idea what he was going to show me, but I did know one thing: I probably didn't want to see it.

"Nice, huh?" Todd asked as we rounded the last corner.

I looked up at the poster we'd put there and drew in a sharp breath.

"At least they left one of them up," Todd said. He was trying to lighten up the situation, but it didn't work. What I was seeing sent chills down my spine, and no amount of joking was going to make those chills go away.

Spray-painted across the poster, in drippy, red, bloody-looking letters, was this message: WILL YOU STILL LOVE ME TOMORROW?

Todd was looking at me as if he expected me to say something, but I couldn't. I was too creeped out.

Read all the books
about **Claudia**
in the Baby-sitters Club series
by Ann M. Martin

THE BABY-SITTERS CLUB®

Stacey

Claudia

Kristy

Mallory

Dawn

Mary Anne

Jessi

Wow! It's really them—
the new Baby-sitters Club dolls!

Your favorite Baby-sitters Club characters have come to life in these
beautiful collector dolls. Each doll wears her own unique clothes and jewelry.
They look just like the girls you have imagined! The dolls also come with their own
individual stories in special edition booklets that you'll find nowhere else.

Look for the new Baby-sitters Club collection...
coming soon to a store near you!

Kenner®